D0502494
NO LONG
SEATTLE

Little Divas

Philana Marie Boles

Amistad
HarperCollinsPublishers

Amistad is an imprint of HarperCollinsPublishers.

Little Divas
 Printed in the United States of America. For information address HarperCollins Children's Books, a division of HarperCollins Publishers, 1350 Avenue of the Americas, New York, NY 10019.

www.harperchildrens.com

Library of Congress Cataloging-in-Publication Data

Boles, Philana Marie.

Little divas / Philana Marie Boles.—1st ed.

p. cm.

Summary: The summer before seventh grade, Cassidy Carter must come to terms with living with her father, practically a stranger, as well as her relationships with her cousins, all amidst the overall confusion of adolescence.

ISBN-10: 0-06-073299-7 (trade bdg.) — ISBN-13: 978-0-06-073299-8 (trade bdg.)

ISBN-10: 0-06-073300-4 (lib. bdg.) — ISBN-13: 978-0-06-073300-1 (lib. bdg.)

1. African Americans—Juvenile fiction. [1. African Americans—Fiction. 2. Fathers and daughters—Fiction. 3. Divorce—Fiction. 4. Cousins—Fiction.] I. Title.

PZ7.B635883Lit 2006 2005005860

[Fic]—dc22

Typography by Sasha Illingworth

1 2 3 4 5 6 7 8 9 10

❖

First Edition

For Jada and Linsey,
our little divas in training.

And in loving memory of one of
my dearest friends from childhood,
Lance Corporal Michael Dale Myers,
United States Marine Corp.
You are forever "Tuna" to me.

June 15

Dear Mom,

Well, you've finally left for Africa and here I am with Daddy. I had a great time with you yesterday—thanks for taking me to the mall. I love this new journal, and I promise to write in it all the time and let you read it when you get back, just like we planned. I know I am going to miss you over the next year, but I'm glad I have good memories to think about too.

You're probably still worrying about whether or not Daddy can handle taking care of me while you are gone, but don't. He and I will take good care of each other. There are already lots of reasons why I think living with Daddy is going to be cool. Want to hear them?

1. My brand-new pink and white canopy bed and all my ruffled pillows.

2. In the morning he listens to funny songs on the radio about liking big fat women and not having enough money to pay the bills. It's called the blues, and Daddy says that B. B. King sings them best.

3. Tonight Daddy watched music videos with me, and he didn't complain once that rap isn't real music. He said that hip-hop is a culture, just like the blues, only it's talking real fast instead of singing.

4. Daddy's new house is so big that I feel like it's a castle, and like I'm the princess.

5. He is the coolest father ever, Mom. I swear! And so are you. The coolest mom, I mean. It's going to be a great year, I promise.

one

"Psst, Cassidy," Rikki whispered as she passed me the mashed potatoes during dinner, "I've got a secret to tell you!"

Now what's the point in telling someone that you've got a secret when you know you can't say what it is until later? Talk about annoying. I just rolled my eyes and kept eating.

Rikki and I are the same age and have been best friends all our lives, but for some reason, this summer we haven't been as close as we used to be. We don't agree on anything anymore. For instance, she can't *wait* to turn thirteen, but me? I'm happy being twelve. And if *I* had a secret to tell *her*, I would just wait until I could reveal what it was before bringing it up.

Later, after dinner we were camping out downstairs in Rikki's basement so that we could help her older sister, Mary, sneak out. Just like Rikki, Mary likes to do what she wants, when she wants, and as often as she pleases. The big difference is that Mary is a whole lot nicer to people in the process, me especially. Maybe that's because she's sixteen and closer to freedom than Rikki and I. I don't know.

Mary was once again sneaking out to see her boyfriend, Archie, and it was taking her forever to leave. I could tell by the way Rikki was acting that she wanted to wait to spill the big, huge, gigantic bowl of beans until after Mary was gone. So, I just tried to think about other things in the meantime, like how Aunt Honey and Uncle Lance's basement is such a funny place.

There's a long lamp with shimmering shingles that reminds me of potato chips. A laundry chute through which dirty clothes come bursting down from the upstairs bathroom is in the back corner. Out of nowhere, *phrump*, you can look over and right there, lying in a basket, will be a pair of Uncle Lance's socks or one of Aunt Honey's bras.

An old floor-model television that we aren't allowed to turn on without permission sits in the corner, along with a stereo that is also a no-no unless Tremaine Hawkins, CeCe Winans, or some other gospel singer's voice is coming from the speakers. Also, there's a shelf lined with old, leather-bound books, which Aunt Honey says are antiques that we're not to touch. It's funny—Rikki and I call this basement our private refuge, yet everything down there is off-limits to us.

I watched as Mary took her time applying her makeup. Annoyed, Rikki tugged impatiently at one of her braids, her dusty-colored hair divided perfectly in two sections with thick yellow ribbons on both ends. She says she's the last twelve-year-old in the world who's still wearing that hairstyle, and I think maybe she's right. Daddy and Uncle Lance are brothers, but Uncle Lance would *never* let Rikki wear her hair down the way Daddy lets me.

I respect that Uncle Lance is a minister and everything, but he and Aunt Honey are so strict that Mary and Rikki say they feel like they're in prison, and honestly, sometimes it really does seem that way. I don't know. Maybe if Aunt Honey and Uncle Lance didn't give us speeches about sinning and damnation and being righteous all the time, my cousins wouldn't stress about growing up so fast.

Still, if I were in their shoes, I'd just wait. Being grown up isn't *that* far off. Easy for me to say, I guess. My parents don't have nearly as many rules as Aunt Honey and Uncle Lance. They don't even live together anymore. As a matter of fact, I moved in with Daddy two months ago because Mom moved all the way to Africa.

I still remember the day Mom announced that she was going to volunteer for an organization called People for Peace. Daddy was dropping me off after a movie, and Mom surprised both of us by inviting Daddy to come in. Something was up. I could feel it. Ever since the divorce a few months earlier, my parents rarely stay in the same room together for long. So when Mom actually asked Daddy to have a seat, I started feeling real nervous, and my throat was tight and dry.

Mom started in by saying that the divorce had helped her

realize how much she regretted not having done some of the things that she's always wanted to do. Then she said that she needed to have "peace of mind" about that. I guess *that's* why they call it People for Peace. Ha, ha.

Anyhow, she was going to be gone for a year, and even though she knew that it would be a tough adjustment for all of us, she needed to know what we thought about me living with my Aunt Beanie while she was away. Daddy immediately called that idea ridiculous.

"Why in the world," Daddy demanded, "should my daughter have to go live with your sister when her very own father is right here in the city?"

"Excuse me?" Mom quickly retorted.

I shook my head, sighed, and closed my eyes. *Here we go again*, I thought.

But actually, I felt just as upset as Daddy sounded. It was one thing that Mom was leaving me for a whole year, but she also wanted me to go live with Aunt Beanie? To share a room with my cousin *Tosha* of all people?

"I'm her father," Daddy reminded Mom. "And if she's going to live with *anybody*, it'll be with me!"

"Well, well, well." Mom made a ticking sound. "Isn't *this* something? Now, all of a sudden, *poof*, you're actually going to have time to be home every evening? So what, me leaving the country is what it's gonna take for you to put down the saxophone, Ray? I'm supposed to believe that you'll actually see to it that your daughter is fed, stays out of trouble, *and* has clean clothes?" Mom chuckled at the thought.

Daddy reminded her that he'd quit the band and wouldn't be touring anymore. He said he'd reserve Saturday nights for gigs and suggested that on those nights I could stay with Uncle Lance and he'd join us at church every Sunday and take me home afterward. How was that?

I opened my eyes, held my breath, and waited. *Please let her say yes. Please, please, please. Puh-leeeeease!*

But Mom laughed at that, too. Uncle Lance had been trying to get Daddy to go to church for years. Was she really supposed to believe that now, all of a sudden, he was going to go *every* Sunday?

Daddy took a long, deep breath and looked Mom in the eye. The room was quiet, without so much as a sigh from any of us as we waited for his answer.

"Yes," Daddy finally replied.

Mom was silent, and still. She didn't so much as blink.

Daddy took a deep breath and spoke a little softer when he said that all he would focus on from then on was being a father. Sure, he was going to start refurbishing the house he'd just bought, and yes, he would have to spend time running the computer repair company he was starting up, but that was it. Maybe their marriage hadn't worked out, Daddy said, but didn't he at least deserve a second chance to be a good father?

Amazingly, Mom was convinced. And boy, was I glad.

And so for the last two months, Mom has been in Africa teaching Ghanaian children to speak English, and Daddy rescued me from having to live with my aunt Beanie for a year. Now I don't have to share a room with my know-it-all, good-goody, oh-so-perfect cousin Tosha. You have to pronounce her name "Toe-shuh," not "Tah-shuh," otherwise she gets upset. Even though she is only a year older than Rikki and me, she doesn't act like it. Tosha goes to a stuck-up, all-girls private school, and thinks she's *so* mature because of it. In June she left to go to some fancy foreign-language camp, so I haven't seen much of her this summer. Not that I care, though. I say good riddance.

So now I only have to put up with Aunt Beanie while Daddy's at work during the week. She watches my every breath and listens out for my every tiptoe, but at least Daddy is home by five o'clock, so it could be worse. And, just like Daddy suggested to Mom that day, on Saturday nights I stay over at Rikki's.

This particular Saturday night Aunt Honey and Uncle Lance were upstairs watching some movie on the USA network, far out of listening distance, and Mary was sitting beside me on the couch. She had just finished applying her lip gloss and was taking a moment to blot. Rikki was eyeing me from the swivel chair she was twisting and turning in, sending urgent glances like she was getting ready to burst open if she had to wait any longer.

"Okay, girls." Mary *finally* sounded as if she were about to leave. "If everything goes as planned tonight, I'll take you down to the Court after church tomorrow. Okay?"

But Rikki looked unimpressed. "What else you got?"

Mary was a little shocked. "What is this, a negotiation?" She laughed.

"Well." Rikki shrugged. "You're the one who wants to go drool all over Archie."

Mary sighed. "Okay . . ." She thought for a moment before snapping her compact closed. "I've got it! How about on my next payday, I'll also take the two of you to the mall? How's that?"

Rikki cut her eyes over at me.

I shrugged. "Sounds cool to me," I said, quite pleased with the results of Rikki's bargaining.

"Fine," Rikki agreed. "That'll work."

"But," Mary said, "that's *only* if you keep me covered until I get back. *Comprende?*" Mary had been teaching us the Spanish she was learning from a girl at the Dairy Queen where she worked. Did we understand, she wanted to know?

"Sí," we agreed.

"And be sure to make at least *some* noise down here, okay? As long as Mom and Dad can hear some Mississippi Mass Choir or something gospel coming from the stereo, they won't bother to check up."

"I know, I know," Rikki groaned.

"Cassidy?"

"Gotcha," I said. Now even *I* was starting to feel eager for Mary to leave. Hadn't we been through this routine a dozen times since she'd started seeing Archie?

Usually Rikki and I pass the evenings by sitting on the floor, our backs up against the couch, looking through Mary's high school yearbook. With pencils, so we can go back and erase things, we like to draw hearts around the faces of guys we think are cute. Tonight, though, I had something else on my mind. The sooner Mary left, the quicker I would get to hear this secret.

Mary sprayed a little peach body mist on the back of her neck. "Just please, don't you *dare* go to sleep until I'm back in the house," she said.

"We know. . . ."

"When I get back"—Mary recapped the plan once more—"I'll go around to the back of the house first. If their bedroom light is off, then I'll know they're asleep. If not, I'll wait in the bushes. You know the signals. One knock on the window means I'm in the bushes waiting—"

Rikki spoke up. "And then we wait for the next signal."

"Right," Mary said. "But two knocks—"

"We know, we know, we know," Rikki interrupted again. "Open the window and let your stupid butt in."

Mary hummed as she blotted her lips once more. "Yeah, I love you, too, little sister," she quipped. "Listen. I just don't wanna forget anything, okay? Tonight is important, and it has to be perfect. So let's see . . . What else?"

"You still haven't told us where you're going," Rikki pointed out.

"That's because I don't know. Just somewhere special where we can be alone." She sprayed another dose of that body spray.

"You big goofball," Rikki snapped. "What if he takes you somewhere and chops you up? How are we supposed to know where to find the pieces?"

Mary laughed. "Please. Archie is a complete gentleman. He would never." Whoa. A third shower of body spray? Tonight must *really* be special.

Suddenly I felt worried about Mary. I wanted to tell her to be careful. But I didn't. I couldn't. Mary looked so excited, especially with the way she kept fixing her hair and slathering more lotion on her arms, so I forced myself to look happy instead. "Have fun," I suggested. I hardly ever say the things that I *really* mean.

Mary winked and gave me a gentle smile. "I will, kiddo. Be sure and wait up for me, okay?"

I watched Mary's brown sandals as she climbed on top of the television, pushed open the window, and crawled out into the dark woods. She'd done this so many times before, but for some reason, just like everything else in my life lately, tonight felt different.

two

Rikki locked the window behind Mary and turned to face me. It seemed too quiet in the room. My throat felt dry, but there was no way I was going upstairs to get something to drink. What if Aunt Honey told me to tell Mary to come up? What would I say? A Carter girl would never tell the truth if it meant getting another one of us into trouble. But I'm nowhere near as good at lying as my cousins are, so I'd just as soon stay thirsty.

"Man, have I got something to *tellll* you." Rikki clasped her hands together. "Are you ready?"

Naturally my cousin had to make a big deal out of making her announcement. She bit down on her bottom lip and took too long to think of the same big, huge, gigantic secret that just a little while ago she'd been dying to tell. Then she pressed her finger to her temple and sat there with a look on her face like she was trying real hard to remember. I hate it when she does that.

"Oh yeah, oh yeah," Rikki finally began. "First of all, do you realize that I had to stay completely still for ten whole minutes for this information?"

I knew that she was exaggerating, but I acted as if I was impressed. "Really?"

"Yes! Mama would kill me if she knew that I was in the hallway eavesdropping."

"Okay," I said. "And so the big secret is . . . ?"

"Mama and some lady were in the kitchen having coffee and talking, right? I don't know who the woman was—couldn't see—but I'm pretty sure that she was from church."

"Okay . . ."

"First the lady asked Mama if she was ready for school to start back up. Mama said 'yes,' but then she said 'and no.'"

"'And no'?"

"That's what she said. She said yes because maybe then me and Mary will stop complaining all the time about not having anything to do."

"And?"

"But then she said 'and no.'"

"Why?" My cousin can be so frustrating sometimes.

"Well, that's when she said that she doesn't know how she's gonna deal with telling *me* about *you* going to private school."

I felt my heart ripple. "Huh?" I said. "Going *where*?"

"Yup. Mama says Uncle Ray is sending you to Clara Ellis."

This time my heart crashed against my ribs. "*What* are you talking about?"

She spoke slowly. "Mama says that Uncle Ray—"

"I heard you," I interrupted. "But, yeah, right."

"Like I would joke about something this serious, Cassidy. Come on."

"Like I said, yeah, *right*."

Rikki sighed. "Sounded to me like it was true."

I dismissed such nonsense. "Yeah, well, I think that I would know about it if my father was going to do something *that* crazy. Don't you?"

Rikki thought for a moment. "But remember how they were with the divorce?"

She was right! Rikki was the one who told me that my parents were separating. Several days before they sat me down in the living room with hot chocolate and graham crackers, telling me in somber voices that there was something that we needed to discuss, I already knew what was coming, thanks to Rikki.

So now what? Was I supposed to wait three days, and then it would be a glass of lemonade and a Popsicle on the porch and Daddy saying, "Cassidy, I've got a major disaster to warn you about"?

This couldn't be happening! Clara Ellis? No!

Rikki said, "Uncle Ray is probably scared to tell you, Cassidy. I bet he thinks you're not gonna wanna go, that you're gonna be mad at him. Just like they didn't know how to tell you about the divorce."

"Uh, *hello*," I shouted, not caring if Aunt Honey and Uncle Lance or anyone else in Forrest Hills heard. "Of course I don't want to go to any stupid private school! Uniforms. All girls. *Tosha!* No way."

Rikki said, "Everybody acts like that school is so great. Like wearing stiff white shirts and plaid skirts every day is a good thing. *Loafers.* Those stupid ugly shoes. Yuck. And having to ride the cheese for five hours every morning? *Humph.*

"I wish my mama *would* tell me that I have to go there. My mama knows better. I'd just hold my breath until I die, right there in front of her. That's why she wouldn't even try that with me."

Barely hearing her, I demanded, "Rikki! Are you absolutely sure that's what you heard? Positively?"

She mimicked her mother's grown-up voice. "'I just don't know how Rikki's gonna handle it, being away from Cassidy. Sometimes I wonder if those two can even breathe without each other.'" Rikki sighed. "Yup. That's what I heard."

Well, I wasn't going to Clara Ellis, that was for sure. I was going to King Junior High with Rikki, and I was going to wake up every morning, sit on a kitchen bar stool, and eat my Frosted Flakes while I watched MTV and waited for Daddy to get dressed. Then he was going to drop me off at King. There would be no yellow bus riding, no standing outside waiting on "the cheese" like everyone at school calls it. I wasn't going to wear a uniform to school every day.

Then I remembered what Rikki and Mary are always complaining about, how as long as you're a kid, your parents get to decide everything for you. What if Daddy really did make me go to Clara Ellis? How could he do this to me?

He had allowed me to wallpaper my new bedroom walls with all the posters I wanted, plus he lets me wear my hair down. I get to buy any lotions and smell-goods that I want from the mall, and all summer I haven't had to have a bedtime. He buys me all the clothes I want, plus CDs, plus anything else. All that, but now he won't let me go to a normal junior high school?

Then again, maybe all I had to do was just tell him no. *Daddy, I'm sorry, but I'm not going to that stupid school. I'm not wearing a uniform. Thank you very much, it was a thoughtful idea, but no.*

I could just make sure to let him know how much I appreciate the thought, that it was really quite nice of him to want to spend thousands of dollars on my education, but I would be just fine going to King. Then I would assure him that I would keep my grades up and stay on the honor role and everything. I just needed to stay calm and talk to Daddy rationally.

After a few moments of both of us just sitting there thinking, Rikki broke the silence. "Please, Cassidy, just don't forget that you're not supposed to know. 'K?"

What? Wait a minute. I was not allowed to talk about

something this devastating, something that had the potential to ruin my life? How in the world not?

But putting that question aside for a minute, I cleared my throat. "Daddy is absolutely cuckoo if he thinks that I'm going to that school, that's all I have to say."

Rikki hummed her agreement.

"Because I am *not*," I insisted.

"I know that's right," Rikki agreed. "I heard the girls there have to keep pictures of boys taped to their folders so they don't forget what they look like."

"Oh well." I shrugged. "Too bad for them."

"I heard that you have to go through a gate just to pull up in front of the school, just to get dropped off."

"And?" I snapped. "So what if you do?"

"Plus, I heard that in gym class you have to ride horses through the woods."

"Let them ride for all I care." I forced a yawn.

"I heard all of the girls there are stuck-up. I heard they're so rich that they arrive every day in private helicopters and fancy limousines. I heard they eat steak and lobster for lunch. And I bet the only music they listen to is classical. *Boring.*"

Even though I knew Rikki was really, really exaggerating at this point, these images made my head pound with tension. "Rikki, did you hear me? It doesn't matter! I am *not* going to that school."

I decided to just concentrate on what it would be like at King. Maybe Rikki and I would have the same lunch period, and I wouldn't need any other friends. Maybe things would go back to being just us—Cassidy and Rikki—the way things used to always work so well.

There were three weeks left until Labor Day weekend, and on the Tuesday after that Rikki and I would have our first day in junior high school together, at King. Yes.

Maybe this year Rikki would even study harder and get switched into honors classes with me. Life would be *perfect* if she did.

"Oh." Rikki had another thought. "I also heard that they make you take a bunch of boring poetry classes. Now you know a school like that has *got* to be stupid."

Then again, who was I kidding? Rikki hates school. And that has nothing to do with whether it's public *or* private. She thinks it's stupid the way I go to the library in the summer when we don't even have book reports to turn in.

So no, things would never be quite perfect, but going to King together would be close enough. I'd settle for that.

"Cassidy," she said through clenched teeth, "do you promise not to tell Uncle Ray that I told you?"

My parents are divorced, and my mother is in Africa. Thanks to a stupid girl named Lane Benson, everybody at school hates me. On top of that, my father is trying to ruin my life. Does Rikki honestly think that I would do anything to make my life even more miserable? I would never be stupid enough to betray my cousin. Nobody wants to lose her best friend, even if they haven't been getting along so well. Best friends are supposed to be forever.

"I won't tell," I pledged.

"Promise?"

"Promise," I said.

"Cool." A look of relief covered her face.

Rikki and I don't cross our hearts and hope to die when we agree to keep something a secret. We don't do any of that extra stuff, silly pinky swears and all that, like some girls do. It's just not necessary for us. A promise is enough.

three

"Where are they? What could they be doing?" I wondered aloud. Mary still wasn't back yet, and it was getting pretty late.

Rikki yawned. "I bet Archie has his tongue in her mouth right now."

Yuuuuuck.

Rikki continued, "All she talks about is how Archie is so different, how he orders his burgers with extra pickles and no cheese. Mary claims that it's the sign of a good man, when he knows exactly what he wants."

Mary has been taking Archie Fuller's order at the Dairy Queen ever since she'd started working there last year. She said that, next to learning Spanish, seeing Archie was the best thing about her job.

"He drinks Orange Crush, no ice," Rikki said, rolling her eyes. "Like *that's* such a big deal."

I punched a couch pillow and tried to situate my neck into a comfortable position. "Why no ice?" I asked. But the truth was, I didn't really care how Archie liked his drinks. How could Daddy consider such a horrible plan for my life without even consulting me? What did I ever do to deserve such a punishment?

I never get in any real trouble. Rikki does. I never say curse words. Rikki does. I never get bad grades. Rikki does. I never get in fights. Rikki does. Plenty. But was anybody talking about sending *her* to Clara Ellis? No. It's not like I do everything right all the time, not like I'm perfect or anything gross like that, but the point is that I'm pretty sure I've never done anything bad enough for a punishment like this!

"I don't know. Probably because it's already chilled when it comes out of the fountain." Rikki was still talking about Archie and his iceless sodas. "Or he doesn't want his teeth to hurt from the cold. You know they're probably already sore from that thing they wear on their teeth. I guess. I don't know. Stupid if you ask me."

"What thing on his teeth?" I asked.

"You know, they shove it in their mouths right before they put on their helmets."

"Oh," I said, pretending to know what she meant.

Rikki put her finger on her cheek and imitated Mary's voice. "Oh, Archie-pooh is so neat. He doesn't leave a big bunch of mess for us to clean up. And all he takes is just one napkin to the table. Not like the rest of the team, those slobs."

Rikki tried to make her voice sound extra dramatic as she continued mimicking her sister. "And I don't care about all those other girls because *I'm* going to be different. Archie is gonna have to work like Paul Bunyan to get even a whiff of the perfume behind my ears." Rikki cracked up laughing.

"What's that mean?" I asked.

She shrugged and rolled her eyes. "Mary said it, so who knows."

"Sounds kinda cool," I said.

"One day," Rikki said, "I'm gonna have a car, Cassidy, watch! A convertible. And we're gonna drive down to the Court. Just me and you. By ourselves."

I imagined Rikki being old enough to drive, and I couldn't help but smile. I pictured us in a convertible, the sun burning highlights into our hair, demanding the red undertones of my skin to appear, the tawny in Rikki's. I bet we're going to be so fantastic when we're sixteen.

To me, imagining is like watching a movie right before my eyes, only it's even better because *I* get to make up the way things look. I pictured me and Rikki laughing, pointing at the boys we thought were cute, and the ones we didn't. Together, we added scenes to our fantasy.

"We'll have diamond tennis bracelets."

"Yeah. Both of us."

"And wear our hair down."

"Both of us."

"Our nails French manicured."

"Fly clothes."

"*Super*fly sunglasses."

"It'll be just us."

"Just me and you."

"That's right."

"Nobody else."

It felt like the good times, like how we used to sit up all night and talk about *someday*. We hadn't done that in a while. It felt nice to do it again. Sometimes talking about doing something is more fun than actually doing it.

Rikki and I used to have so much more fun. We used to do regular stuff, like riding our bikes all day but going nowhere, and really silly things like catching lightning bugs and peeking into our clasped fists to see if they would glow in the dark. Life used to be all about ponytails in the morning and who cares how it looks for the rest of the day. We used to play with Barbies. Now we both carry purses with tiny mirrors and tubes of lip gloss tucked inside. Sometimes I wonder if I'm the only one of us who has noticed these changes, though, because none of it seems to bother Rikki. All she cares about anymore is boys.

Upstairs was completely still. Aunt Honey and Uncle Lance must have been good and asleep by then. I asked Rikki, "Don't you think it's taking Mary a long time?"

"No," she said.

"You're not nervous? Not even a little?"

She rolled her eyes. "Please. Why should I be? She's the

one that Daddy's gonna punish for the rest of her life if she gets caught, not me."

"I mean, don't you just hope that she's okay?" I said. "It's getting late."

"Well, it's my parents' fault if she's not. Won't let nobody be a real teenager around here. Shoot. If she is dead, what're they gonna say to the judge? Because I'm gonna tell him—'It's their fault, Your Honor. My parents are too strict!'"

"You ever think about how Daddy and Uncle Lance are so different?"

"You mean how Uncle Ray is normal, and my daddy's not. Duh!"

"Yeah, but at least Uncle Lance isn't trying to send you to Clara Ellis," I reminded her.

"Well, that's only because he knows that I'd just run away if he tried." Rikki hopped off the couch and headed over to the washing machine. She started fumbling around behind it, and I sat up, knowing exactly what she was going over there to do. It was *not* to wash a load of clothes.

Contraband.

Rikki had written the word in graffiti letters, with a capital red *C*, across the top of one of Uncle Lance's old boot boxes. Mary buys us peach Jolly Ranchers, watermelon Hubba Bubba, Wet 'n' Wild glitter fingernail polish (and remover to erase the evidence), *Teen Vogue*, *Seventeen*, and *YM* magazines, playing cards, and grape Lip Smackers to store inside our Contraband container. We keep the box hidden behind the washing machine. Rikki is smart. She and Mary do all the laundry, so how will Aunt Honey ever find it?

Rikki and I sat facing each other with our legs folded, and she pulled out our sixth-grade class photo. Darwin Mack, Sam Woods, and Travis Jones were in the last row on the end, and all three of them had their arms folded across their chests, with their chins lifted in a what's-up expression.

Rikki touched Darwin's face and said, "Me and Darwin are gonna get married someday. Watch."

I sighed. "Well, I hope Travis isn't at the wedding. Because if he is—"

"We won't invite him," Rikki easily agreed, tossing the picture back in the box and pulling out a deck of cards to begin a game of solitaire.

A few months ago at the end-of-year sixth-grade carnival, I'd decided that I never again in life wanted to see or speak with Travis Jones. One of our classmates, Lane Benson, had been proclaiming all year that I was stuck-up. The day of the carnival, she said that if I wasn't, I had to prove it, and according to her, the only way I could do that was to kiss a boy. She picked Travis Jones.

A small crowd had gathered, including Travis, and I'd never felt so alone. Only students who hadn't gotten into any trouble during fourth quarter, no detentions or anything, were allowed to come to the carnival, so Rikki wasn't there. She isn't afraid to tell *anyone* how she feels, and grown-ups are no exception, but you get detention for talking back to teachers, so Rikki almost always has to stay after school. If Rikki were at the carnival, she *never* would have let Lane Benson terrorize me like that.

No matter if Rikki and me get along or not, we're cousins first, and defending each other to outsiders is what being family is all about.

I tried to imagine what curse words Rikki would have used, but usually, whenever I try them, they come out sounding corny. At least that's what Rikki always says. So I didn't dare try. The only thing worse than feeling stupid is actually *sounding* like you are.

With every breath that I tried taking, my heart pounded harder. My palms were so moist that I was losing my grip on the plastic bag containing the goldfish I'd won. Already I'd named him Goldie.

Shantal Henry, who had also won a goldfish and had been standing beside me, was inching away now, trying to blend into the blur of the crowd. I should've never bothered to go to that stupid carnival in the first place, at least not without Rikki, and definitely not with Shantal.

I swallowed hard, *real* hard, and looked around. One, two, three . . . Altogether there were eight of my classmates watching, waiting to see if I was going to faint or take the challenge.

Lane folded her arms across her chest, twisted her lips, and declared that I had to kiss Travis Jones, a short, ashy, brown-skinned boy with freckles. If I didn't, she was going to call me stuck-up every time she saw me for the rest of our lives.

There was no way, I mean *no no no* way, that I was going to waste my first kiss on Travis Jones. Lane Benson and the rest of her training bra crew could kiss all the boys in the entire school if they wanted, for all I cared. I had more important things to do.

At a school assembly a few months before, a skinny, stern-looking old woman from Tomorrow's Achievers had spoken to us about goals and dreams. Most of it was boring stuff we'd already heard from our parents and teachers, so I didn't perk up until I heard her say the words "in conclusion."

"As you continue on into your teenage years," she said, "as you go off next school year to junior high school, please remember to start setting goals, and to keep your eyes glued on them."

Travis, who was sitting behind me, snickered, more than likely at the idea of eyes being glued.

She continued, "The choices you make today will affect you for the rest of your lives. You can choose to play today and have to work hard in the future, or you can work hard *today* and play as much as you want when you become an adult."

I started daydreaming at that point, imagining myself grown up, cruising the lake on a sailboat with friends, laughing and drinking fancy champagne. Rikki would be there, too. . . .

But then Travis's raspy voice snapped me out of it.

"Shoot," he said, "who wants to be old, still playing freeze tag?"

There was no way that I was going to waste my first kiss

on the silliest boy in school. No thank you.

But there Travis stood at the carnival that day, waiting with his hands stuffed in the pockets of his baggy jeans, and with a goofy grin on his face that showed his crooked teeth. He nodded his head up. "So what's up?" he said.

Yuuuuuuck.

I wanted to lean over and vomit.

"Come on, Cassidy," Travis said.

I felt the plastic bag slip out of my hand and heard a quick pop, followed by the quiet *shhhh* of water pouring onto the grass. Looking down was out of the question. I did not want to watch as my new pet, totally defenseless, gasped for his final breaths. I knew just how he felt. No air. Unable to breathe. Terrified, with absolutely no one there to help.

No matter how hard I tried, even though I desperately wanted to do so, I could not get my hand to form into a fist. Rikki always had a way of making that look easy too.

Lane looked me up and down real slowly, like the sight of me was making her feel nauseous. With one hand on her hip and the other holding the cherry-flavored lip gloss that she'd been applying nonstop for the last two years, she offered a dry laugh. "Anybody want fried fish for dinner?"

The whole crowd crackled with laughter.

And they *kept* laughing, and laughing, and laughing. I wanted to punch all of them, each and every one, *especially* Shantal, that traitor! There was nothing even funny in the first place.

The bottom of my right foot felt damp inside my sandal, and I had to bite down on my bottom lip in order to stop it from quivering. I glared at Travis Jones, who was laughing the loudest.

Somehow, though, I managed to put one foot in front of the other. Going toward home, the farther away I got, the louder their laughter seemed, and the more my eyes burned with hot tears. I never wanted to see any of them again. Ever.

"Cassidy," Rikki said now, sensing how tense I'd become. "I know how you feel. But I honestly think that Travis likes you. Maybe you could just give him a—"

"He's annoying," I reminded her.

She shrugged, and with her voice noticeably softer, she said, "Okay."

"*All* of the boys at school are annoying," I said. Then I snatched up a *Jet* magazine and started flipping through it. I stopped when I came across a picture of some actor, whose name I couldn't recall, but I knew he was starring in a new flick about a college marching band. I pressed my thumb against his face and turned it around so that Rikki could see. "Now he's cute."

She nodded, but didn't seem all that interested.

I flipped through the pages some more. "Let's make our boyfriends work hard too, okay?"

Rikki laughed a little. "What do you mean?"

"You know," I said. "Like all that stuff that Mary said. Before they get to smell our perfume . . ."

"Oh," Rikki said, reaching for a pack of banana Now and Laters. "Right. Of course. Not even a *whiff*." And then a grin appeared on her face. "Yeah, we're gonna make them sweat."

Tap. Tap.

Finally! Another one of Mary's rendezvous, as she likes to call them, had gone off without a hitch. Rikki, I was sure, was going to see to it that Mary made good on her end of the deal. And as Mary crawled back through the window, I hoped that she had made Archie work like Paul Bunyan tonight, just like she'd said she would. Whoever that was. Whatever that meant.

August 13

Dear Mom,

The whole summer has been absolutely great. Daddy and I have been pretty busy with going to church every Sunday. I'm sure he'll be there again tomorrow morning, as a matter of fact. Oh, and Rikki and I are getting along just fine.

School is starting in a few weeks, and I can hardly believe it. It's pretty weird to think that I'll actually be going to King Junior High School! Can you believe it? Me. Cassidy Jane Carter, going to King! Yup.

Daddy made scrambled eggs, Bob Evans sausage, and sourdough toast with grape jelly for breakfast this morning. Isn't he doing a great job taking good care of me? I think so too.

Hope they have real food like eggs and sausage where you are. Hope you're having fun being so far away!

four

The next morning every head was bowed, including mine. In silence, the entire congregation was thinking about all the people that it wanted God to bless. Easy for me. I prayed for the same people every Sunday.

Aunt Honey . . . Uncle Lance . . . my cousin Mary.

When I prayed for my uncle, I asked God to let his sermon make people shout today. Church was always so much more fun when someone did. Sometimes, especially when Uncle Lance got real excited and started sweating a whole lot, or when he started talking extra loud into the microphone, I too would feel the urge to jump up, throw my hands in the air, and shout out to the heavens. But I never did. I just liked to watch.

I felt Rikki tap my leg.

And my other cousin too, Lord. Please help Rikki Renée Carter to be quiet when we're told.

It's not that I didn't want to talk to Rikki, but there are some pretty simple ways to avoid getting in trouble in life. Not talking during prayer is one of them. Things are just so much easier when you don't have your parents fussing at you about something.

"Hey," Rikki whispered. "Hey, Cassidy."

I cleared my throat, closed my eyes tighter, and did not reply. Ignoring Rikki, I kept going with my prayers.

And Daddy, too, Lord. Can you do something special for him? Maybe send him down a real nice surprise so he'll stop thinking about sending me to Clara Ellis? Like maybe that shiny white and gold saxophone in Harmony's window, the one he drives past and looks at when they're closed. Or maybe a new dog. We could teach him how to play dead, and how to howl at the moon like he's singing. That'd be nice. Well, whatever you think, just would you please send it? Please?

Then I prayed for Mom.

My mother—Lord please don't let her catch any strange diseases and don't let her get attacked by any wild animals. And don't let her be too sad about missing me, okay?

"Amen, amen, amen!" Uncle Lance was at the podium now, and his voice boomed out of the speakers. "Can the church say amen?"

"Amen!" the church called back. And then a few phrases like "Praise the Lord" and "Glory be to God" trickled after.

I glanced over my left shoulder and looked two rows back. Daddy looked so handsome in his white shirt and blue tie. He smiled at me and winked. So far Daddy hadn't missed a Sunday. Everything had been going so well. So why was he trying to mess everything up with all this business about sending me to Clara Ellis?

I shifted back around in my seat, and the pew made a noisy creak, so I concentrated on being still. Rikki sighed and grabbed one of those three-inch eraserless pencils that are always in the wooden pockets on the back of every pew. My cousin will do anything to avoid listening during church.

Don't get me wrong, I wouldn't like having to go to church more than just on Sunday mornings either. Mary and Rikki have to go several times a week! Still, though, what's the use in complaining or acting up? All that ever gets us is a lecture.

As the seven-member choir started warming up, the swaying of their bright puffy yellow and green robes seemed to brighten the room. Uncle Lance, who is also the pianist, sat down, tapped on a piano key, and nodded his head enthusiastically as they got ready to begin. With his round upper body and the way his head just seems to sit, *kaplunk*, on top of his head, Uncle Lance reminds me of a walrus.

On an envelope intended for tithing, and in her bubbly handwriting, Rikki handed me a note that was only one sentence long.

We're saying we're going for ice cream. 'K?

I knew what this meant. Once the last offering had been taken, after the prayer of dismissal had been fastened with a unanimous "amen," we would head over to the Court.

A few Sundays ago Rikki's note had said the library. The week before that it had said the mall. Today it was ice cream. We can never reveal to Aunt Honey and Uncle Lance where we really like to hang out, because there are always lots of boys at the Court. They'll just take it upon themselves to come by and check up on us for sure. Mary and Rikki would rather croak than have that happen.

From the corner of my eye, I could see Rikki twiddling her thumbs, and noticed she was trying real hard not to grin. My stomach tightened. Didn't she know I had other things to worry about than going down to the Court to look at boys?

Maybe once Uncle Lance started his sermon, he'd get on a roll and make it take a long time. Maybe it would be close to dinner by the time we left.

I folded the note and placed it in the pocket of my jean skirt. Then I looked over at the pink floral print of Mary's ankle-length skirt. Her right hand was holding a key chain that she'd purchased at a gas station, and a picture of a rose garden was staring back at me. Mary saw me looking and smiled. When she got her driver's license a few months ago, Uncle Lance bought her a new white Chevy Cavalier. It's *supposed* to be for nothing more than getting her back and forth to work at the Dairy Queen, although occasionally Mary convinces her parents that she's taking me and Rikki somewhere safe, for a good reason—someplace where we can't get into any trouble. Yeah, right.

I turned my attention back to the choir.

"Do not.
Do not.
Doooo not pass me by!"

The resounding voices seemed to be growing more excited as they sang out a plea to the Lord not to forget about them during His return to collect worthy souls for Heaven. The funny thing was, with their happy smiles and cheerful eyes, none of them really looked concerned.

After church Daddy, Rikki, and I were waiting outside on the sidewalk for Uncle Lance and Aunt Honey, who had to stand in the lobby and greet members of the congregation. Mary was already in her car, talking on her cell phone and waiting for Rikki and me. Even though I had agreed to ride home with my cousins, really I just wanted to go home with Daddy. But a promise is a promise, and I still couldn't say a word about the secret.

I especially didn't feel up to riding in Mary's car today, with Rikki cutting me one of her you're-so-stupid looks if I accidentally sang along to whatever song was playing on the radio. Rikki almost always rolls her eyes at me when I do, and then she'll sing louder, her way of laughing at me without so much as a smile. She's a great singer.

Standing next to me, Rikki had plastered a huge grin on her face as she pleaded with Daddy to let me spend the night again. "Okay, Uncle Ray?" she begged. "Please, just one more night? Please? Pretty please? With sugar and a cherry on top?"

Daddy laughed, but I didn't see anything funny. The real reason Rikki was clinging to Daddy's arm had absolutely nothing to do with her wanting to spend some more time with me. She just needed someone to talk to while Mary flirted with Archie at the Court. Boys. That's all anyone cared about anymore, especially Mary. She's hopeless.

I was hoping that Daddy would say that I couldn't go. Maybe if I went home, he would sit me down with that glass of lemonade. Then I could plea my case. But Daddy just gave me his usual kiss on the forehead and a crisp five-dollar bill, and then he told me not to ruin my appetite before dinner. Ruin my appetite? How about ruining my life! He still hadn't said anything about me not going to King!

Maybe Aunt Honey didn't know what she was talking about. If Daddy were planning on making me switch schools, wouldn't he have said something before now? School was starting in just a few weeks. I mean, not that it mattered. I was going to King whether he said something about it or not, but still.

"Thanks, Daddy," I said halfheartedly as I tucked the money into my purse.

"You're welcome, pumpkin," he said. Then he smiled at Rikki. "You're quite the charmer, you know."

Rikki giggled, and then her foot jerked out and hit mine. She gave one of her ponytails a determined tug, and I knew that that was body language for how excited she was that her plea to Daddy had worked.

"You're too cool, Uncle Ray," Rikki said.

Uncle Lance and Aunt Honey *finally* joined us on the sidewalk, and Uncle Lance sure looked tired. His thick, bushy eyebrows, coal-black ones just like Daddy's and mine, were hunched together, but he tried to look pleased. "Good to have you with us again, Raymin," he told Daddy.

"Good to be here," Daddy replied proudly.

"Join us for dinner, Ray?" Aunt Honey suggested. Mary and Rikki get their creamy, coffee-colored skin and warm brown hair from her. That day Aunt Honey was dressed in a svelte purple suit and shiny black pumps with skinny heels, but I knew she was anxious to get out of her church clothes, to go home and let her hair fall out of its bun. She likes to sit down somewhere and "prop her feet up" like she always says, but not before preparing a huge Sunday dinner.

Daddy said that he was going to have to pass, but thanked her for the invitation. Since I was staying the night again, that would give him time to go home and get caught up on some paperwork. He reminded me to be on my best behavior before heading toward his Cadillac.

I didn't dare tell Rikki that what I really wanted to do was go back to their house and chill, maybe watch a *Cosby Show* marathon on Nickelodeon or something. Rikki would have called me stupid if I'd have said such a thing, and when she calls you stupid, she definitely has a way of making you feel like you actually are.

When we were out of earshot of Aunt Honey and Uncle Lance, Rikki tugged at my arm, leaning in close enough that I could smell the watermelon Hubba Bubba on her breath. "I bet the Court is gonna be packed today," she said.

Rikki climbed into the front seat of Mary's car, and I securely fastened myself in the back. Just as we were getting ready to drive off, Uncle Lance flagged Mary down and she pulled the car up to the curb. Uncle Lance's eyes were narrowed. "Home by seven o'clock," he said, eyeing Mary's unbuckled seat belt. "And I mean it."

Mary snapped herself into safety. "I know, Daddy," she said, her voice sounding overly sweet and innocent.

But Uncle Lance was still a little hesitant. "And I thought you said you were tired of looking at ice cream? 'Daddy, all I do is look at ice cream all the time,' that's what you said."

Mary gave him one of her big innocent smiles. *"Oh, Daddy,"* she sang. "This is different from work; it's just for fun. Just kicking it with my little sisters."

I always feel a tingle of pride when Mary refers to me as her little sister. Being an only child, I feel kind of happy to think of having a big sister, especially one as nice as Mary, even if it is just pretend. I've never one time in my life heard

Mary call anyone or anything stupid.

Uncle Lance opened his billfold and reluctantly counted out a few dollars. "You ask me, ice cream is ice cream."

No, it isn't, Uncle Lance. No, it isn't.

five

My teeth were clenched so tight that I was getting a headache. The whole way over to the park, Rikki kept looking over her shoulder at me, building up some anticipation like we were getting ready to have the time of our lives.

Officially the park's name is Grace Nelson Park, but you only know that if you look for the wooden sign at the entrance. Over the years the name has become less and less visible because the two bushes on either side of it have gotten so plump that they are closing in on the words. Now all you can see are the letters "son Par."

Everything goes down at the center of the park at the bottom of a long hilly road. Mostly it's just a big wooden jungle gym, a long row of swings, a huge teeter-totter, a few tire swings, and a small pond full of ducks. But the *real* reason why on any given day in the summertime every person under the age of eighteen makes their way down there, the magnet for everyone, is the basketball court. It was pretty crowded that Sunday.

Mary parked at the top of the hill and turned off the ignition. Once our ears got used to not hearing music, we could hear the laughter from down the hill, the jive talkin', and insults spiked with occasional curse words. Every few minutes bass could be heard from a car cruising through the lot.

Archie wasn't there yet, but he would be. He's older than Mary, a senior to her junior, and he's very cute.

We heard a loud thump and some shouts and looked down the hill to see that two boys had fallen on the basketball court. Both of them were cursing out loud. Rikki gasped when she saw that the one holding onto the basketball was Darwin Mack, the object of her obsession. But he got up, brushed himself off, and started playing again. It looked like there was a little blood on his knees, but that didn't seem to matter; such things never do down at the Court.

Rikki smacked her lips. "Who knocked down my baby? Don't make me have to go down there."

Mary strained to see. "Sharee Jones's little brother, it looks like."

Rikki and I looked at each other, and said at the same time, *"Travis?"*

Mary stared some more. Then she shrugged. Matter-of-factly she said, "Yeah."

I shook my head at the possibility.

Yeah, right.

"Travis Jones is not that tall," Rikki said.

"I don't think so," I agreed. "No way."

After glancing at the red Ford Escort parked a few spaces over, Mary insisted, "Well, that's definitely Sharee's car. I'm sure he probably rode with her."

Rikki said, "Travis isn't that dark, either."

"Or that tall," I noted, even though Rikki had already pointed this out.

Mary had an answer for that, too. "Well, you know they spent most of the summer in California with their grandparents. So, with all that sun . . . You know, he probably just grew."

"Wait a minute," Rikki said as she squinted. "I think that *is* him."

No way.

I still did not think so.

Uh-uh.

Rikki nudged me. "Maybe laying out on the beach in all that sun *did* make Travis darker."

"Who cares," I snapped. "He's still ugly."

Rikki sighed and rolled her eyes. "He likes Cassidy," Rikki informed Mary.

"Awww," Mary sang. "That would be *so* cute, Cassidy. My little sister and Sharee's little brother. *Awwww* . . ."

Yuck.

And just then, I couldn't believe it. The boy who I thought

was way too cute and way too tall to possibly be Travis made a basket. He threw his hands up in the air and did a stupid victory dance, the exact one that Travis always does in gym where he moves his neck back and forth like a duck. I did not want to believe my eyes, but Travis Jones was almost as tall as Darwin now. How in the world did that happen?

Rikki laughed, also recognizing the duck dance. "That *is* him!"

"Go tell him hi," Mary suggested. "Ask him how Cali was. Maybe he met someone famous. Maybe he's got autographs. Maybe he's got pictures."

I was so annoyed that I felt my teeth gritting. "Who really cares if he does?"

"Cassidy *hates* Travis," Rikki explained. "He killed her goldfish."

Swoosh, Darwin's shot from the three-point line went in, all net.

Rikki started clapping. "Look at Darwin down there ballin'. Come on, Cassidy, let's go. I should go down there, be like Cheryl Swoops, Lisa Leslie or something. I bet I can hoop too if I try."

Disgusted, Mary sighed. "Would you stop with that tomboy stuff, Rikki. *Please?*"

Heavy bass announced the arrival of a four-door Buick Park Avenue. When it pulled up beside us, Mary started squealing.

"Hop in the back," Mary instructed Rikki.

As if she didn't already know what to do.

As if she wasn't already doing it.

All the Buick's passengers, varsity football players, got out and headed down toward the pond. I watched as they stopped to talk to a group of girls sitting down at a picnic table.

Archie Fuller was real cool, one of the few popular boys who was smart in school. Mary says that's because he's a football player and he *has* to get good grades. He's not allowed to suit up if he doesn't.

Today he was wearing a maroon T-shirt with a picture of a growling bulldog on the back, his nickname, "Arch," ironed on in thick white letters. He got into the Cavalier and closed the door, and the cool, breezy scent of his cologne or aftershave or something filled the air. Immediately Archie started adjusting the passenger seat, until it was pushed up against my knees.

"Is that too far back?" he asked.

Mary glanced back at me, pleading with her eyes.

So even though my knees had the weight of a stack of dictionaries pushing back against them, my answer was no. "I'm okay," I said.

Mary looked relieved, but Rikki rolled her eyes. Now *she* was disgusted.

"Come on, Cassidy," Rikki said. "Let's go down to the swings."

Mary had another look in her eyes this time, softer, but still pleading. I really did want Mary to be happy.

"Fine," I told Rikki as I peeled my knees off the leather on the back of the seat.

I would walk down by the swings, but *not* by the basketball court, not anywhere *near* that Travis Jones.

Once we were a few feet away from the car, Rikki smacked her lips. "Now that we're gone, I bet Mary's in the car gettin' all poetic on Arch."

I actually thought that Mary's poems were beautiful, better than most of the ones at school, that's for sure, the boring ones that are in our blue and gray literature books. I folded my arms across my chest as we walked down the grassy knoll and didn't say a word.

On my first Saturday night at Aunt Honey and Uncle Lance's after Mom left, I had a terrible nightmare. I dreamed that Mom was behind a big, scary-looking waterfall, and she couldn't get to me. Because of all the water, I couldn't see her face too good. And even though it was a dream, I could feel the cool, misty breeze and the beads of water popping against my face. The water was making Mom look like a milky-white ghost.

The strangest part about that dream was that the closer Mom got to me, the more terrified I became. I must've been crying in my sleep, because the next thing I knew Mary was sitting on the side of Rikki's canopy bed, shaking me, frantically trying to wake me up. She was holding me, asking me what was wrong, and telling me it was going to be okay.

Rikki was on the other side of the bed with the pillow over

her head, groaning that she was trying to get some sleep, but Mary's voice was a caring whisper. "It's okay, Cassidy. You just need to wake up."

My face was damp, and my teeth were sore from clenching.

"What was it?" Mary stroked the side of my face. "What were you dreaming about?" She wiped the tears off my face.

"I dreamed that I couldn't see my mother. And she was trying to get to me, but she couldn't." As soon as I spoke the words, panic struck again, and I had to sit straight up. "I can't remember what she looks like," I said. Even being wide awake, I still couldn't picture my mother's face.

Mary continued rocking us both back and forth. "Shhh . . . shhh . . ." she said. "It was just a dream, Cassidy. Think sweet thoughts now."

And so I did. Eventually I could remember Mom's face, her round cheeks, and even that tiny mole at the corner of her left eye. It even started to sound as if Mary's voice was Mom's, and finally I began falling back to sleep.

The next morning, beside my pillow, there was a beautiful piece of lavender stationery covered with Mary's flowing handwriting in thick black ink.

> Like a tulip in winter, a snowflake in spring
> Seems so impossible that her splendor be seen.
> But her face, her beauty, eternally you'll see.

For just last night, so clearly reflected,
was she on your face while you rested
A mirror reflection, always, your mother,
she will be.

As Rikki and I continued down the hill, I thought about how I had paper clipped the poem into my journal, but didn't write anything down about my nightmare. I just wanted Mom to see how beautiful Mary's poem was.

Maybe I'm not being totally honest when I write in my journal, but I promised Dad that I would try not to make Mom feel bad about leaving. Plus I don't want Mom to come back and read that things were rough, especially between Dad and me. She'd just think she was right after all. Then again, with this Clara Ellis thing, maybe she was. Maybe things would be different if she were here. I don't know.

The Court is always a pretty good illustration of how diverse Forrest Hills is. At school, at church, and no matter where you live, our city is so mixed that no one ever really feels like a minority. It seemed like all the kids in the city were there that day, like a kaleidoscope of races. Like always, everybody, no matter who you were, just wanted to have fun.

"Look," Rikki said under her breath.

It was pretty boy Darwin Mack, and he had just finished with his game. Now he was waving his arms in the air. "Yo! Rikki!" he called.

I winced when I saw the smile on Rikki's face. Great. Just great.

Rikki undid her braids, pulled all of her hair back into a big, bushy ponytail, and started walking real slow. "Let's go on over there," she said.

As usual, I saw no choice but to follow.

Six

Darwin was sitting on top of a picnic table with two other guys watching a new game. I tried not to look at their faces just in case one of them was Travis. I did not want to accidentally make eye contact.

When we reached the table, Darwin said to Rikki, "Man! Took you long enough, walkin' all slow," he teased.

Rikki hit his leg and quipped right back, "What? I'm supposed to run, just 'cause you're here?"

Darwin swiveled his legs over and Rikki sat down in front of him. "Uh, *yeah*." Darwin laughed. "You know you wanted to."

"Boy, please."

Darwin's face was shiny with sweat from his basketball game, and he was sipping from a can of Faygo Red Pop. After taking a gulp, he looked at me and smiled.

"What up, Cassidy?" he said. "I see you got your hair down. That's tight."

I smiled back. Darwin was probably the coolest guy at school, and I doubt he's ever had an enemy.

"Thanks," I replied.

Rikki teased him. "Yeah, we saw you out there hoopin' like a straight-up klutz. I know your knees hurt."

Darwin laughed. "At least I can dribble."

Rikki nudged his legs with her back. "I *do* know how to dribble, fool."

Darwin took another sip of his Faygo. "So, what's up? Ya'll comin' to my party?"

"What party?" Rikki asked.

"My house," he said. "A pool party. We passed out the fliers earlier. A week from next Saturday. S'up?"

Rikki cleared her throat. "I love the way you saved us a flier. That was *so* nice of you. You *really* want us to come, don't you?"

"My bad," Darwin replied with his winning grin. He turned to one of the other guys sitting at the table. "Yo, T. Money, we got any more of those fliers?"

As I sat down on the end of the bench, I felt someone jump off the table, and he stood in front of me. I forced myself to look down at the grass, already knowing who it was.

He held out a lime-green, crumpled-up flier, and waited. Finally I looked up, and I smacked my lips the way Rikki does.

Taller and a lot better looking weren't the only things about Travis that had changed over the summer. He was smiling, and I could see that he'd also gotten braces on his teeth.

"Here. It's the last one." One thing hadn't changed yet—Travis's voice was still as raspy as ever. Rikki reached over and snatched the flier out of his hand and started reading, but he kept looking right at me.

"Comin'?" Travis wanted to know.

I shrugged.

"Yes," Rikki answered. "We are."

Darwin said, "From, like, noon till whenever. But no swimsuit, no party. None of that wearing regular clothes, dipping your toes in, and being stuck-up all day stuff. Everybody has to get in the pool. Bet?"

I felt the heat from Travis's stare, felt the pierce of his sneer without even having to see it. I cut my eyes at him, dared him to say a word in front of Rikki, then again hoping in a way that he *would*. It'd be nice to watch him get punched.

But, surprisingly, Travis wasn't smirking.

He said to me, "Your hair really does look tight, Cassidy."

I dug the tip of my toes into the mound of dirt underneath the bench. Maybe if I ignored him long enough, he'd just go away.

Rikki hopped up and told me she'd be right back, and I watched as she and Darwin locked hands and started off on a stroll together. I wanted to scream at her. How could she leave me like that?

Travis sat down right next to me, and I honestly wanted to

bawl. I bit down on my tongue and decided to just concentrate on basketball. But when I looked over at the Court, I could see that a game had just ended. It would probably be a few minutes before another one started up.

Travis broke the silence. “Man, that’s whack. I can’t believe it’s only three more weeks until we have to go back to school.”

I didn’t say a word. I wished that he would just be quiet.

He said, “You comin’ to King?”

“Of *course*,” I snapped. “Why wouldn’t I?”

“Dang!” He looked confused. “My bad. I was just asking.”

Sam, the other boy who was sitting on the table, hopped down and walked over to get in on the new game.

Now it was just Travis and just me.

Alone.

Why?

Why?

Why?

He tapped my arm. “Yo, Cassidy . . .”

I yanked my arm away even though he was no longer touching it.

“Whoa,” he said, visibly shocked by my reaction.

I sighed.

“For real, though,” he said. “Why you gotta be so mean all the time? On everything.” He kinda laughed.

“I am nice,” I snapped, “to people who are nice to me.” It was as if my heart was pounding in my neck and even in my ears. I scooted away from him. Why wouldn't he just leave me alone? Why was Travis Jones always playing around?

He reached down into his sock and pulled out a few folded bills. The one on top was a ten.

"Went to California this summer," he said, "worked in my grandfather's garage. Made a whole lotta money, too."

Was this supposed to impress me? I folded my arms across my chest. Now I couldn't possibly care less if I ever saw or talked to Rikki ever again in life. How could she leave me alone with Travis like this?

"Why so quiet?" he asked.

I didn't answer.

We sat in silence for a few moments.

Eventually he spoke again. "You want some ice cream?"

Was this really Travis? The same boy who used to throw paper airplanes across the room when Mr. Middleton wasn't looking? Who used to take straws and blow paper balls at people during lunch? I looked at him, tried to make sense of it all, but couldn't. What had happened to him?

"Come on," he said, a tiny glimpse of his braces showing through his half smile. "It's 'bout ninety degrees out here." He stood up and waited for me to do the same. He even had on crisp new tennis shoes.

I sat there waiting for the joke to come, wondering if he was going to take off running and laughing if I actually did stand up. Maybe he was going to try and trip me when I started walking.

"Man, come on," he insisted with a laugh that sounded a bit nervous. "For real. Before the truck leaves."

And so, grudgingly, and definitely full of suspicion, I walked with him over to the yellow ice cream truck that was parked behind the basketball court. Neither of us said a word while we waited in line, but when it was our turn, Travis spoke to the old man who owned the truck.

"Let me get two of them ice cream bars," he said. But then he turned to me. "Cool?"

I shrugged. "I don't really like ice cream bars."

"They got Push-Ups," he suggested.

"A cherry freeze," I decided.

"Make that one ice cream bar," he told the man, "and a cherry freeze, then." The freckles across his nose were still there. His eyes were the same. But since when did Travis Jones act this pleasant?

He paid for our snacks and handed me mine, and we walked back to the table. Travis took a big huge bite and started talking with his mouth full. *That* was definitely a Travis thing to do.

"So you comin' to the pool party or what?" he asked.

I shrugged.

"It's gonna be tight," he said. "We already started making some mixes. We got all the new cuts and everything."

I slurped up some of my cherry freeze.

"So, um," he said after a while of just listening to the sounds of us eating, "when you gone let me get that kiss?"

I jerked my head to look at him. "*What?*"

He laughed a little. "You don't remember when you left me hangin'?"

I started pumping my legs back and forth underneath the bench. "You don't remember when you killed my fish?"

He chuckled. "I know you're not still mad about your little homey."

Through clenched teeth I said, "My little *homey*?" I looked away and felt myself beginning to seethe as I thought about what he'd just said.

I *definitely* still hated Travis Jones.

"Look." He nudged me. "On everything. You're the one who dropped him."

"Yeah, but whose fault was it that I did?"

"Not mine."

I jumped off of the bench and started walking away.

"Man," he called, "where you going?"

I spotted a green plastic garbage can and dumped the rest of that stupid cherry freeze right into it.

Travis cracked up laughing and called out, "That ain't even cool, Cassidy. Man, where you going?"

I didn't answer. Because I didn't know.

It was beginning to feel like forever. I'd been sitting on the hood of Mary's car for a really long time before Rikki *finally* found me.

"Have you seen Mary?" I demanded as soon as she was

standing in front of me.

"Down there." Rikki gestured with her thumb back toward the Court. "Watching Archie hoop."

"Well, I'm ready to go," I said.

Rikki laughed a little. "So why are you sitting up here mad?" she asked.

"I'm not."

She shook her head. "I asked T. Money where you went and he's like, 'Man, I don't know. Man, she trippin'.'"

There are so many times when I wonder whether or not I would like Rikki at all if she weren't my cousin. *This* was one of those moments. I decided then that I would not.

After she'd gone around to the passenger side of the car and unlocked the door, I crawled into the backseat and sat there with my arms folded across my chest, with my mouth in a pout, and determined not to answer.

"Ooh," she started in. "Darwin is—"

"Don't talk to me." I stopped her before she started in on her bragging.

"Dang," she said. "What's wrong with you?"

"You left me," I reminded her. "Alone. With Travis, of all people."

"Because, look. Darwin whispered in my ear that T. Money was—"

"And why do you keep calling him that? His name is Travis Jones."

"Naw, Darwin said everyone calls him T. Money now."

"That's stupid."

"So, look," she continued. "He was like, 'T. Money is trying to holler at Cassidy, so why don't me and you step away for a minute, give 'em some space.'"

"And you actually did it? How could you, Rikki?"

"You're really mad, aren't you?"

"I cannot believe you did that to me."

"My bad."

"Whatever."

"But Travis *is* cuter now, ain't he?"

"Who cares, Rikki? *Who* cares?"

"He said he bought you some ice cream," she pointed out.

"So."

"Well, maybe   "

"Where'd you go with Darwin?"

"Over by the pond."

"I cannot believe you left me."

"We gotta go to that party, cool?" Rikki twisted around to face me. "If Travis messes with you, I'll knock him upside his head. We *have* to go to that pool party, Cassidy."

"I'm not stopping you."

"Everybody is gonna be there. Forget Travis. Oh, and guess what?"

"What?"

"Darwin said that Lane Benson is going to Clara Ellis this year too."

I felt a pang in my chest. And then I remembered that it

didn't matter if Lane Benson was going to another school. In fact, it was a good thing that she was going to Clara Ellis, because *I* was going to King.

Maybe things would be more different this year than I'd ever imagined. With Lane Benson gone, maybe Yolanda, Whitney, and even that shady Shantal would start talking to me again, let me eat with them at lunch like we all used to before Lane turned everybody against me. Maybe I wouldn't even need Rikki.

I saw Mary making her way back up the hill, and I could not possibly have been any happier.

Rikki saw Mary coming too, and said, "Here she comes."

But I was determined to sit in silence.

With a hint of desperation in her voice, Rikki said, "Come *on*, all right? We have to go to that party, Cassidy. We'll say we're going to the library, 'k?"

I exhaled. "Like I said, you don't need me to go."

She was quiet for a moment. "Okay. Fine, then."

Silence. And more silence.

"Cassidy, come on," she eventually started in again. "If I see Lane Benson, with her giraffe-looking self, I'll pop her."

"I am ignoring you," I sang.

Rikki turned back around in a huff. "You know what? I *will* go by myself. I'm not gonna beg you."

Mary got in the car, saw both of us with our arms folded across our chests, and immediately wanted to know what was wrong. Neither of us answered.

In fact, the whole time Mary rebraided Rikki's hair, the car was silent. And the whole way home, too. Tension between Rikki and me never lasted long, but this time I wasn't so sure it was going to blow over.

August 17

Dear Mom,

This is still the best summer ever, for the most part. Daddy is doing everything he said he would. Going to church, fixing up the house, and working. That's it. On top of that, every night he and I do something fun together. Last night we played Bingo on the sunporch.

I think me living with Daddy was a great idea, Mom. Don't you? It's not that I don't love Aunt Beanie, but I don't know if she's doing so well. In fact, I wonder if she's sick, a brain tumor or something. Whenever she's over here, it seems like all she does is rub her temples. But whenever I ask her what's wrong, she just shoos me away, groans, and tells me, "Nothing. Not a thing. Just go on somewhere."

Hope you're not too scared of all the elephants and zebras running around. Hope you're not staying up late wondering if I'm okay. I am, for the most part.

Seven

After a few days Rikki and I were still a little sore at each other, but we were talking again. That's just the way we are. I still couldn't believe she'd left me alone with Travis, but it was even worse being alone with Aunt Beanie all day, so I was glad that Rikki had asked to come over. We were jump roping in front of Daddy's house, and Aunt Beanie was huffin' and puffin' from the front porch, lookin' like she could blow a house down.

"Ya'll know better than to be swinging those hips like that!" she yelled.

Only two and a half more weeks until Labor Day. Only two more weeks of Aunt Beanie. Thank goodness.

Daddy was working late and had asked Aunt Beanie to keep an eye on us. And boy, was she. She looked like she wanted to march down to the sidewalk and snatch us up, like she wanted to pop us one real good. But I knew she wouldn't. Aunt Beanie just likes to fuss.

Daddy's house is in the city, about ten minutes away from the dirt and gravel roads where Aunt Honey and Uncle Lance live. It's a renewed historic neighborhood near the forest of trees that our city is named after. With restored houses that are so big that they look like mansions, you'd think all the people who lived in this neighborhood were filthy rich, but really it's upper middle class. Most people buy these houses as fixer-uppers. Daddy is doing a great job on his. He just painted the outside white and the shutters dark green, and it looks very clean and new.

He says he wants to build a kitchen upstairs and rent that out as a one-bedroom apartment someday. The house is *that* gigantic. Rikki and I like to sneak upstairs and pretend we're the ones renting it, like we're roommates in a big city, fancy apartment together. We act like we have famous boyfriends with fancy cars parked outside. Sometimes we put our hands to our faces and pretend we're making phone calls.

Hello, this is Cassidy/Hello, this is Rikki . . . Can you please have our private jet sent up to the roof? We'd like to leave for Italy in an hour.

The house where Mom and I live is closer to the center of town. It's a moderate-sized, beige, three-bedroom, all on one floor, with a fenced-in backyard. It seemed much bigger after Daddy moved out. Still, it's tiny compared to his new house.

I looked up from the sidewalk and wondered how come Aunt Beanie never realizes that that big bouffant wig of hers is always crooked. Then again, maybe she knows and just doesn't care. I wonder what her hair is really like under there.

A hard, cold glare had set in Rikki's eyes as she looked at Aunt Beanie, and I knew just what was coming.

But Aunt Beanie fired a look right back. "Out here acting like you're twenty-one going on thirty," she said. "God's gone get ya'll."

Well, in that case, He was going to punish every girl between the ages of ten and eighteen living in Forrest Hills, because we all sing these songs. Rikki and I had just gotten sloppy, had forgotten to keep our voices down to a hush. Even Aunt Beanie's goody-goody daughter, Tosha, knows the words to that song. I could have told Aunt Beanie a whole lot about that daughter of hers, the one that she thinks is oh-so-perfect. But I didn't say a word because

1. I am Ray Carter's daughter, which means that I am a Carter girl, which means that I am loyal. A Carter girl must never ever tattle on *anyone*. Ever.

2. Being labeled stuck-up can be a real bad thing, but being known as a rat is just flat-out planet doom. This is another reason why nobody likes Tosha.

Rikki put her hand on her hips and yelled back, "Oh yeah? Well, God's gonna get you, too, Ms. Beanie."

Aunt Beanie reared back and widened her eyes.

Rikki continued, "Gluttony is a sin too, you know."

Aunt Beanie gasped.

"That's right," Rikki persisted. "How many of them cinnamon coffee cakes you eat today, Ms. Beanie? Three? Or was it ten?"

Aunt Beanie's words came out slow and steady, like air seeping out of the tip of a balloon. "You'd . . . better . . . watch . . . it . . . little . . . girl."

"Watch *what*, Ms. Beanie, how much food you eat?"

Aunt Beanie gasped again, louder this time. "Talking to grown folks like that! You keep on, you little sassy, no-manners-havin', mean little youngster, you."

I watched Rikki fold one of her arms over the other as her trademark satisfied smirk appeared. Gripping the jump rope I was holding, I silently hoped that Rikki was not about to cuss. *Oh Lord, please, no.* Anything. A fat joke. A wig joke. *But please don't let Rikki say a curse word.*

I wanted to stop Rikki, to beg her not to say another word, but that would've been like holding your hand out in front of a tornado and politely asking it to stop. All I could do was brace myself.

Rikki shook her head back and forth. "Ooh," she said, "I'm gone tell my mama what you just called me. I'm tellin', I'm tellin'. *And* I'm gone tell my uncle Ray."

Aunt Beanie reared up, looked like she was about to say something, but then she just shook her head and frowned like she was utterly disgusted.

A few long, tense seconds later, Aunt Beanie's nostrils were flared open and beads of sweat were pouring down her puffy cheeks, and she looked right at me.

"Cassidy Carter," she said, like *I* was the one who'd just sassed her, "ya'll not gonna give me a headache today, you hear? I'll just wait until your daddy gets back here. I'm gonna tell him just what ya'll was down there singing about, too. You just wait until your mother calls."

Rikki rolled her eyes, snatched the rope from me, and started jumping solo.

Aunt Beanie has this way of looking people up and down and breathing so heavy at the same time that it seems like the very sight of you is making her angry. Mom always says that that's Aunt Beanie's way of sizing people up, and that's just how she was looking at me.

"If you ask me," she said, "that daddy of yours *does* need to send you over to Clara Ellis Academy. That's just where you need to be. Watch me tell him so, too."

That made Rikki miss a jump. And me a breath.

"That's right," Aunt Beanie said. "I said it."

We had definitely gotten on Aunt Beanie's last nerve at this point. I knew because when she stormed into the house, she let the screen door slam. Aunt Beanie *never* leaves me unattended.

So it *was* true! Daddy *was* trying to ruin my life! And so not only had he told *Aunt Honey*, but he'd told *Aunt Beanie*, too, probably even the whole city of Forrest Hills, Ohio! Maybe he'd talked to everyone in the world about this before me.

Rikki grunted, and I looked over to see a bright red spot on her leg where the rope had burned her shin. She smacked her lips. "Look what she made me do." She shouted out her favorite curse word, making me extra glad Aunt Beanie was gone from the porch.

But Aunt Beanie reappeared in the living room window with her eyes squinted and a look of complete satisfaction on her face. Having just caught Rikki in a major sin, Aunt Beanie lowered her chin, narrowed her eyes, and gave a slit of a smile before she stepped away from the window.

Rikki groaned. "Made me peel my leg. I'm tellin' Daddy."

She wrapped the pink and silver jump rope tight around her hands, planted her feet, and said, "She needs to mind her own business. Big fathead."

"Did you hear what she said?"

"Nobody's listening to her, Cassidy."

I sniffed, but didn't say anything. I had kept my promise to Rikki and hadn't said a word to Daddy. But the fact that Aunt Honey and even Rikki knew about something so major before I did really, really bothered me.

"That woman always has something to say," Rikki said. "She makes me sick. Her and that irritating daughter of hers."

"I know," I said, but my head was cloudy with confusion.

Daddy had told *Beanie* before he told me, the very person whose life he was going to ruin? Instead he'd told the very person that he and I had joined together and pleaded with Mom not to make me go live with?

Rikki said, "That's why she's chubby and ugly, because she deserves to be."

Hearing Rikki say this made me think about those songs on the radio that make Daddy smile, even laugh out loud sometimes. Songs about big fat women, the man singing about how he wanted a big woman to be his wife, a woman so big that only one of them would be able to fit in the front seat of the car. He said a skinny woman couldn't do anything for him. Only a dog wants a bone, he said, and it *buries* that when it gets one.

This made me want to laugh, and I thought about telling Rikki about that song. But I knew she wouldn't grin and snap her fingers the way Daddy and I do. She'd just say it was stupid. Plus, on second thought, that's a pretty hefty woman. Only room enough for one person in the front seat of a car? Man. Whoa.

Rikki's face was impatient as she handed me the other end of the rope. "Twirl," she instructed me.

I tied one end of the rope to the mailbox, while Rikki tightened her ponytail. And then it was on. But I was so distracted by Daddy's betrayal that I twirled extra hard this time. I was never going to listen to that blues station with him ever again. Never. Ever!

I like coffee. I like tea.
I like Darwin, and he likes me.
Shimmy-shimmy cocoa puff.
Shimmy-shimmy swirl.
I know he loves me,
'Cause I'm the cutest girrrrl. . . .

Rikki could do the swirl part so good. She could go way down to the ground, still twirling her hips like she was hula hooping, all the while jump roping. But this time she missed.

My extra strong twirl made the rope hit the scrape on Rikki's shin. Immediately it produced a stream of blood that raced down to her white cotton socks.

She muttered something and snatched open the flap on the lime-green purse that was hanging down across her chest. Then she sat down to apply pressure with a Kleenex.

I joined her on the ground, pulled my legs into my chest, and began apologizing.

She didn't reply at first, just kept wiping and wiping.

I gazed out across at the galaxy of trees throughout the neighborhood, and I started wishing I could fly. Far, far away, way above the trees.

Daddy has always seemed so much more normal than Uncle Lance, but maybe he isn't. Maybe he, too, thinks that what he says goes and that his daughter's opinion doesn't really matter. Maybe on the first day of school he's just going to hand me a stiff plaid uniform and say, "Here. Put this on. You're not going to King. Off to Clara Ellis you go."

I felt the heat of tears coming and tried to focus on counting the trees. I had only gotten to twenty-nine when my eyes got blurry, and I had to blink away the aching in my chest.

Rikki was rocking back and forth, like now all of a sudden she was in tremendous pain.

"You all right?" I asked, even though I knew she was doing better than me. *I* was the one who was not okay. Rikki should have been asking me.

"I can't *wait* to go back to school," she said.

Rikki had a chronic case of the couldn't waits. She couldn't wait to turn sixteen, couldn't wait to drive. She couldn't wait for Mary to turn eighteen, and couldn't wait to go live with her when she did. She couldn't wait until she, too, was grown, and she was leaving Ohio first thing when she was.

Now she couldn't wait to go back to school.

She said, "I hope Darwin is in every last one of my classes." And of course, she couldn't wait to find out.

I stared out into the acres of trees and felt my eyes burning again. What if Daddy did make me go to Clara Ellis? What would I do? Tosha. Lane Benson.

I'd run away. I'd go live out there in the woods with nobody to bother me except maybe a friendly deer every once in a while, a quiet bird looking for a worm down by my feet, or an occasional squirrel to feed.

I sighed, and began wondering what kind of trees Mom was looking at right then. Was she okay? Was she afraid? She'd sounded so happy on the phone the other night. She'd gone on and on about how rewarding her trip was, how when I'm older she's going to take me back there so that I can experience true humanity. I had tried to sound cheerful, but in a strange way it was weird that she didn't sound at least a little bit sad. She sounded *extra* cheerful, in fact, and it seemed like her voice was coming from so far away.

We didn't get to talk long. Mom asked me if I'd been writing in my journal, and I told her I had. I told her that when she gets to read it, she is going to be amazed at how much fun I've been having. I would too, she said, when I read hers.

I continued staring at the trees, partially lost in my own thoughts, partly listening to Rikki still complaining.

Only a couple more weeks left of summer vacation. Soon the leaves will fall. The trees will be nothing but plain old brown and naked twigs. And *still*, Mom would be gone.

I closed my eyes and swallowed the anguish I felt.

The more I thought about Daddy telling Aunt Beanie before talking to me, the more furious I became. I didn't know if I ever wanted to talk to Daddy again. In fact, I was pretty sure I didn't.

Rikki kicked a pile of gravel rocks. "Maybe I should be a gospel singer."

"You could," I said with a sniff. "If you really wanted to."

"What are you gonna be?"

I thought for a moment. "I don't know," I said. "I guess I never really thought about it."

"You're always writing in that journal of yours. You could travel the world and write about fabulous places."

"Maybe," I said.

"As long as we're important in the world."

"Definitely," I agreed.

"And can go wherever we want, whenever we choose."

"Yeah," I agreed.

"As long as we're *respected*," Rikki added. "You know what I mean? I want people to know my name when they see me coming. I want 'em to salute me."

I thought about that. "I think I'd rather just be rich," I concluded. "Not famous."

"Still, we'll have our own private airplanes and everything."

"Every day I wanna wear white linen suits and high-heeled shoes with open toes."

"And walk down a red carpet that's been laid out especially for me."

"Blowing kisses to the crowds of people."

"Lane Benson is gonna be begging you for your autograph one day, Cassidy. Watch."

"Sorry," I said, and then blew on my fingernails. "I don't have time."

"Not for stupid idiot girls. That's right."

"Yeah . . ."

"I can't wait to grow up," Rikki said. "And to be able to make my own decisions about my own life."

"Me either," I said. For the first time ever, I knew *exactly* how Rikki felt.

"Look at Mary. She still has to sneak around to see that big fathead boyfriend of hers."

I felt bad for Mary, always on constant lockdown. You'd think Aunt Honey and Uncle Lance would at least let her have a little more of life now that she's sixteen. She's practically an adult.

"I bet if Mary was ugly," Rikki said, "they wouldn't make her stay all cooped up in the house like that. Bet if she looked like Tosha, they'd be *hoping* a boy would look at her. It doesn't say anywhere in the Bible that kids aren't allowed to have boyfriends. If Mary ever does run away, I swear I'm going with her."

"I'm going too," I said without hesitation.

Rikki sulked some more. "But yeah, right. And go where? Everywhere you go in this little bitty town, somebody knows your parents." She stood up, brushed the gravel off her backside, and looked up the street. "We'd probably only make it down there to the corner before somebody would see us and call our parents."

Rikki gazed down the street, and I got up and let my eyes follow hers. Forrest Hills. One of the smallest cities in Ohio, where it really seems like everybody's parents know every-body else's.

I had just started humming my agreement when we saw a big orange and white U-Haul truck coming our way.

eight

Two hours after we saw the moving truck pull up, Rikki and I were sitting on Daddy's front porch watching as the movers went in and out of the house to the left of us. We'd been sitting still so long by now that the plastic lawn chairs were stuck to the backs of our thighs. I hate it when that happens.

A few weeks ago Daddy and I had noticed that the "For Sale" sign in the lawn next door was gone. He'd said then that he bet that the new people were going to move in just in time for school, that they probably had kids. More than anything, I was just hoping they'd be normal. The neighbors to the right of Daddy, the Thompsons, are not.

The Thompsons own and operate a funeral parlor with the help of their grown children, and I am terrified of their entire family. I never look at them if they're outside. Rikki says that their hands probably smell like dead people, and there is *no way* I am ever getting close enough to find out.

After a while Daddy's Cadillac came rolling up the street. When he pulled into the driveway, he had a great big old grin on his face and threw his hand up to wave. I didn't think there was anything in the world to be smiling about, and I did not wave back.

Just how long did he think it would be before I found out about his underhanded little idea, anyhow?

Daddy stood in our driveway for a moment and looked over at the moving truck. "See anybody yet?" he asked us.

Rikki nodded at a boy standing in the driveway who looked like he was about fifteen years old. His hair was dirty blond, his body too skinny, and his skin pale. He was twirling on the string of a red yo-yo. "Just weird-o over there," Rikki said.

Daddy looked over to the boy and hollered, "Welcome!"

The boy looked up, blew the hair out of his eyes in order to see Daddy, glanced at the moving truck, and then at their opened garage. "Thanks," he mumbled back.

Still grinning and loosening his tie, Daddy came up the steps. "Well, well, well," he said. "What have my little girls been up to today?"

"Hey, Uncle Ray," Rikki said.

I just glared.

"Whoa." Daddy saw the look on my face. "You okay?"

I could hear Aunt Beanie inside, mumbling and fussing as

she came closer to the screen door. "Is that you, Ray?" she called.

"I'm here," Daddy called back. "I appreciate you staying over, Beanie. Sorry it took so long."

Daddy slid off his tie. "Everything okay, pumpkin? You look bothered."

I stared up at the skyline and bit down on my tongue. I thought I could speak at first, but when I tried, I couldn't. It was all just too much even thinking about it.

Daddy shifted a bit and cleared his throat. "Rikki?"

But she just shrugged.

"Daddy"—my voice cracked as I finally spoke—"how could you?"

Rikki tapped my foot.

"Hey, hey," Daddy said with a concerned voice. "Look at me." He was silent as he waited for me to do so. When I finally did, he searched my face and my eyes real hard for a clue as to what was troubling me. "How could I do what?"

"I can't believe you, Daddy. I can't believe you would do this to me. Away from all my—"

"Whoa." Daddy held up his hand. "Pump the brakes."

Aunt Beanie was standing in the doorway listening. "I apologize, Ray," she said, "but, Cassidy, go on and tell your daddy what you did. She made me say it, Ray."

He looked at Beanie, at Rikki, and then back at me. "Well? I'm waiting."

"Because we were jump roping," I said.

"Yeah," Rikki added with a huff.

Beanie shrieked, "And what else? That ain't all, Ray!"

I folded my arms across my chest. "Oh, what difference does it make? Aunt Beanie said that you're sending me to Clara Ellis."

Daddy used his thumbnail to scratch his forehead and waited a moment. Then he sighed. "Well, we did receive a letter from the school at the beginning of summer, right before your mother left. We thought about it, but it was never more than a consideration, Cassidy. That's all."

I titled my head and stared. "Daddy."

He actually looked a little nervous. "Yes?"

"What do you mean the 'beginning of summer'? Are you telling me that everyone else has known about this since—"

"Now, now, look here. Clara Ellis sent a letter regarding your aptitude test scores. Your mother called me to discuss it—"

"What?" I sat straight up. "*Mom* knew?"

"All right now, you need to watch your tone of voice."

"But Daddy! Mom knew and didn't say a—"

"Now listen. There was no point in telling you. We didn't want you to get excited and then—"

"Excited!" I shouted. "Do you honestly think I would be *excited* about going to that stupid school? That I wouldn't want to go to King? That I don't—"

"Well." He smiled a bit. "You *are* going to King, pumpkin.

That's what matters, right? Clara Ellis was merely a consideration."

"But you discussed it with everyone in the whole world, even Aunt Honey—"

Rikki took a real deep breath.

Oops.

Daddy got a strange look on his face and looked over at Rikki. "Did your mother say something to you about this?"

"No," I answered before Rikki could. "Daddy, see! You're not even listening to me. I said I bet you *probably* discussed it with Aunt Honey. I said you *probably* told—"

But Daddy was still looking at Rikki. He raised an eyebrow. "Rikki, I'm going to ask you this again. Did your mother say something to you about this?"

Rikki shrugged and shook her head. "First I've heard of this was today, Uncle Ray," she said. "When Miss Beanie said it."

Daddy looked like he wanted to discuss the matter further, but just then a Volkswagen station wagon pulled up and parked behind the U-Haul next door. A woman emerged from the driver's side, and a girl with long dark-blond hair got out of the passenger seat. The girl went inside the house without even looking our way, but the woman bounced right over to our porch and stood at the bottom of the steps.

"How do you do?" she said in a way that reminded me of a camp counselor. Her blonde hair was cut into a bob and moved easily when she talked. Her big brown eyes were bright and cheerful as she scrunched up her nose.

"Raymin Carter." Daddy walked down the steps and shook her hand. "Welcome."

"Kate Anders," she replied. "Thanks. Good to meet you."

"Can we offer you a glass of lemonade?"

"Oh. Thanks. I've got my water bottle. I thought that if we waited until the sun went down, we'd avoid some of the heat. Silly me."

"Yeah, seems like the humidity stays out with the moon these days," Daddy said.

She stuffed her hands into the pockets of her shorts and smiled at Rikki and me like we were cute little baby dolls or something. "These your little girls?"

"Yup," Daddy said. "The one on the left is my daughter, Cassidy. And the one on the right is Rikki, my niece."

"Oh, great." Mrs. Anders grinned.

Daddy cleared his throat and laughed a little. "Uh, don't let the frowns fool you. They're nice young ladies, good girls."

Mrs. Anders seemed to find that amusing. "Well, then. I am pleased to meet all of you. That's my son over there with the yo-yo. Freddy. Give him a skateboard and a yo-yo and he's happy. I've got a daughter, too. She's inside." Mrs. Anders gasped. "And *I bet* she's the same age as you girls."

Daddy nodded. "Great, great."

"I'm divorced," Mrs. Anders explained to Daddy, "so the kids, you know, they're adjusting."

"I see," Daddy said. "Same here."

"Will your girls be attending King Junior High?" Mrs.

Anders asked Daddy.

Daddy laughed a stupid, goofy-sounding laugh. "As a matter fact, yes," he said.

"Oh, great!" she exclaimed. And then she put her hands on her knees and bent down to talk to Rikki and me. It was just like my first-grade teacher used to do, like if she sounded really excited we would be too. "Would you girls like to come meet my daughter? I just know you'll be great friends."

I heard Rikki groan under her breath.

"Sure they would." Daddy winked at me. "That'd be the neighborly thing to do. Right, girls?"

Mrs. Anders beamed. "Shall we?"

The Anders house was big like Daddy's, but it was blue with white shutters and had a brick walkway up to the front door. Except for neatly labeled boxes scattered throughout, the inside was hollow.

The floors were all hardwood, and most of the walls were painted a pale yellow. We walked upstairs, and Mrs. Anders gently pushed open a bedroom door. The walls in there were yellow, too, but a brighter shade. The person who'd lived here before sure must've liked yellow. It was the perfect house for Mrs. Anders, I thought, such a happy color throughout. I couldn't imagine that there was a single day in her life when Mrs. Anders wasn't smiling, she seemed *that* happy.

The girl who'd gotten out of the passenger side of the Volkswagen was sitting in the middle of the floor with her back to us, her legs folded and her face buried in a book.

Mrs. Anders's perky voice seemed too loud in the silence and too delighted for the somber mood in the room. "Golden, honey!"

"Hmmm?" The girl didn't even bother to look up.

"I'd like you to meet your new friends. Turn around, okay?"

Rikki rolled her eyes at that. There was no *way* she was going to be friends with this girl, and I knew it. I could tell that Rikki did not like Mrs. Anders thinking that we were already friends with her daughter, but for some reason I didn't mind so much.

Mrs. Anders said, "I just know you three will get along great."

The girl glanced up then, but she just stared straight ahead at the wall.

"Honey," her mother insisted. "Turn around, now. I'd like you to meet Cassidy—she lives right next door—and her cousin Rikki. You'll be going to school with them. Right, girls?"

"Right," I said quickly.

Golden finally turned around.

She was very pretty, and I imagined that if she smiled she'd be even prettier. Her skin had an olive glow, and she looked just a little older than us. But perhaps that was only because of the shiny pink lip gloss she was wearing.

A slit of a smile appeared on Golden's face, but in the next second her round cheeks deflated again. She ran her fingers through her hair and ruffled it a bit before she said in a low voice, "Hey, Rikki. Hey, Cass."

And with that, she turned back around. She looked down and turned a page in the book she was reading.

I thought that was so cool, the way Golden felt free to give someone she'd just met a new nickname, the way it had so easily rolled off her tongue, no second thoughts, just like that.

I hadn't forgotten how Mrs. Anders had mentioned to Daddy that she was divorced, and that her kids were still "adjusting." A part of me wondered if maybe Golden's parents used to argue a lot too.

I wasn't opposed to the idea of staying awhile longer and getting to know Golden, but Rikki was tapping her foot again. She was irritated and ready to go, so we said good-bye and left. I'd have to find a reason to come back and talk to my new friend later.

August 20

Dear Mom,

I have a new friend and her name is Golden. Her family just moved in next to Daddy, and she is the same age as me and Rikki.

Now I just *know* the school year is going to be fun. Hopefully Rikki and Golden will hit it off, and the three of us can be best friends. Actually, it was Daddy who suggested that I make friends with Golden. Wasn't that a good idea, to be neighborly?

Things are still going great this way, Mom. I hope you're not missing Wendy's too much. I know how much you love those Frostys. I don't think they have fast food in Africa. Ah, well. Maybe you can get some in a year.

Nine

A couple of days passed, but I couldn't forget about my parents' betrayal. So, when Mary took Rikki and me to Jacobson's to look for bathing suits, I told Daddy we were going to the library. Hey, he'd kept things from me, so maybe it was time that I do the same.

It should've been a fun day, but Rikki was having a fit. "Forget that," she said to me as she flipped through some hangers, shaking her head back and forth. Then she stopped, cut her eyes at me, and glared with such intensity that it made me want to back away from her. Usually only the laws of Aunt Honey and Uncle Lance made Rikki *this* angry, so I knew I'd messed up.

Rikki said, "Just because she's your stupid little neighbor doesn't mean you have to be nice to her, Cassidy. This *ain't* TV."

I had only seen Golden twice since the day she moved in, and both times her hair had been in a messy ponytail, her bangs hanging sloppily over her eyes like her brother's. Each time she'd been alone. I thought she might be lonely.

Yesterday I'd been sitting on the porch reading a Judy Blume novel when I saw her come out of the house and run down to the mailbox at the curb. I wanted to say something to her, but she grabbed the mail and hurried back into the house so quick that I didn't have a chance.

This afternoon, while I was sitting on the porch waiting for Mary and Rikki to come pick me up, I saw her again retrieving the mail. I made it over to her just as she was walking back up the driveway. She was sorting through the envelopes.

"Hello," I said.

She looked up, but didn't smile. "Oh." She nodded and blew the hair out of her eyes. "Cass, right?"

"Cass." I smiled. "Right."

She thumbed through the mail and held up a flat blue envelope that was covered with lots of stickers, mostly puppies and horses. Quite a few stamps were in the upper right-hand corner. "My pen pal," Golden informed me.

"Oh?"

She nodded. "She lives in Italy. We send perfume with our letters." She held the envelope up to my nose to smell, and I did. It was a soft scent, pretty and delicate like a flower garden.

"That's nice," I said, and inhaled once more before she took it away. "Very nice."

"I sent her Exclamation last month," she said.

"My cousin Mary has that!" I said.

"It's so cool."

"I know," I said.

I didn't know what else to say after that.

Golden tapped the envelope. "Her name is Isabella. She's fourteen. I wasn't sure if she'd gotten my new address yet. How old's Mary?"

"Sixteen."

Golden nodded. "I have a sister who's sixteen."

"Cool!" I said. "We can introduce them. I'm sure Mary would show her around school and stuff."

"Oh." Golden shrugged. "Well, my sister doesn't actually live with us right now."

Golden looked over at her house, like she'd much rather be inside than continue talking, so I changed the subject.

"Rikki's on her way over," I said. "We're going shopping."

"That's cool," she said dryly.

"For school clothes," I told her.

"Nice," she said with forced enthusiasm.

"And bathing suits," I added.

For the first time Golden's face lit up. "Really?"

"Do you swim?"

"We had a pool at our last house. And the house before that."

"How many houses have you lived in?" I asked.

She shrugged. "Four. But who's counting?"

"Well, our friend is having a pool party," I said. "He's going to King too." Darwin, I was sure, would be nice to Golden.

"Cool," she said, and even smiled a bit this time.

I didn't even think about consulting with Rikki first. It just came out. "Wanna come?" I asked.

"Sure," she said. "When is it?"

"Next Saturday. I'm staying the night at Rikki's afterward. My aunt Honey and uncle Lance are unbelievably strict, but all we have to do is tell them that you want to go to church with us on Sunday, and I bet we can convince them to let you spend the night too."

But now, in the middle of the "Miss J." department at Jacobson's, Rikki was throwing a fit. Like it would just ruin her life to be nice to someone for a change. She couldn't believe I'd asked Golden to join us, and now she was threatening to never speak to me again. She went to the other side of the clothing rack, still fussing, still slamming hangers around.

She said, "That girl doesn't even bother to comb her hair."

Mary overheard Rikki and a look of annoyance crossed her face. Uncle Lance had gotten Mary a cell phone—in case of road emergencies only—but yeah, right. Mary had been talking nonstop to her best friend, Dierdre, for at least a half hour now, going on and on about how much fun she and

Archie had had talking on the phone the night before. She told Deirdre to hold on a second.

"Rikki," Mary said, "Cassidy's right. It won't kill you to be nice to the new girl. Now would you please just pick out a suit?"

Rikki ignored Mary, who went back to talking on the phone, and said to me, "It needs to be just me and you at that party, Cassidy. Remember? The way things work best. Now can we please just shut up talking about that messy-haired girl?"

With that, we were done discussing Golden.

Rikki picked out a suit the same color as her skin, creamy, coffee colored and soft. She fell in love with it as soon as she saw it on the hanger, but once she tried it on, she *had* to have it.

"Everyone's gonna think you're naked," Mary said after finally hanging up with Deirdre.

"Like they can't see these ties hanging down off my shoulders," Rikki said. "Ain't nobody that blind."

"I know, but—"

"You said *whichever* ones we want," Rikki reminded Mary.

"I know, but—"

"Well, I want it." Rikki's face was set.

"It's just the color . . ." Mary countered hesitantly. "It looks too much like your skin."

"Well. It's the one I want," Rikki said.

If Uncle Lance could have seen his daughter right that

very second, he would have had a fit. He would have laid holy hands on the salesperson for allowing that suit to be sold in their store, then he would've given Rikki—all three of us, probably—a sermon on sinful desires.

But the swimming suits were top-secret gifts from Mary, and none of us would ever tell.

Mary looked at me. "And what about you, kiddo?"

I had my own money, so Mary really just needed to buy one for Rikki, but Mary insisted on buying my suit too. She was proud of her earnings from making ice cream sundaes and those delectable flurries with the crushed Snickers, and she'd said that she liked spending money on us.

I held up a lilac suit with satin ruffles on the top that I'd been eyeing and tried to glance at the price tag, but Mary took it from me before I could.

"*This*," she said as she eased the suit from my hands, "is a splendid choice, Cassidy. A ladylike color. And it's so demure, just like the princess who'll be wearing it."

Mary has the graceful vocabulary of a poet much older in years. Mundane words, she always says, are repulsive, absolutely *lazy*.

"Mary," Rikki said, "it's not like I really *care* if you don't like mine. Just so you know."

A faint smile appeared in Mary's eyes. "I like yours, too, Rikki. It's a little risqué," she said. "But who cares? It's fun."

Mary was excited to pay for those suits. I could see it on

her face, like there was something satisfying about having such authority.

"Look," Rikki said to me as Mary exchanged small talk with the sales clerk. "All I'm saying is what if she embarrasses us?"

Apparently Rikki had decided that we could get back on the subject of Golden.

Now it was my turn to roll my eyes. "How would she do that, Rikki? She's nice. She even has a pen pal in Italy."

"And I thought you said you didn't want to go to Darwin's party in the first place?"

"Well, I do," I said. "I just don't want to see Travis."

Rikki thought for a moment. "What if she snorts when she laughs?"

"She won't," I moaned. "Come on, Rikki."

"What if she wears an ugly suit?"

I sighed. "She won't."

"What if she stinks?"

"She doesn't," I said. "She wears Exclamation. Like Mary."

"Well, what if she talks too much?"

"She hardly talks at all," I reminded her.

"Well, I don't like her."

I sighed again. "Please don't tell me it's because she's white?"

"I—don't—like—girls—with—messy—hair—and—weird—brothers! I wouldn't care if she was green."

I considered that for a moment. I honestly doubted that it

would make a bit of difference to Rikki if Golden were any other color. Rikki doesn't have a single friend besides me. And Darwin, of course, but that's it. There just aren't too many people that Rikki likes, no matter what race they are.

I said, "Well, at least you could try to get to know her, Rikki. She seems cool."

"I *don't*," Rikki said, "want to. And neither should you."

But for once I didn't really care *what* Rikki said. I'd already asked Golden to go with us. And an invite is an invite.

ten

On the way home Mary pulled up at a corner store and gave us five dollars to stock up on goods for our contraband box. As Rikki and I were getting out of the car, Mary was already dialing the phone to talk to Archie.

As we started walking up the sidewalk, Rikki started humming.

I ignored her.

But then she broke out into laughter.

I turned to her. "What's so funny?"

"Bet you don't know what I know," she sang as we approached the entrance to the store.

I was starting to detest Rikki Renée Carter! I was tired of always having to beg her to tell me something, so this time I didn't even bother to respond.

She put her hand on the door just before I could. "Don't you wanna know?"

I put a hand on my hip. "Why should I, Rikki? So you can just say that you'll tell me later?"

She looked a little bothered. "Well, all I was going to say was that I heard something about Uncle Ray."

I put my other hand on my other hip. "What do you mean you 'heard something' about my daddy? Kinda thing is that to say?"

I reached for the door, but Rikki wouldn't move.

Still, I put my hand on the door handle too. I had as much right to open up the door as she did.

"For real," she said. "I heard Mama on the phone this morning. She said that Uncle Ray went out to dinner with some woman last week. Ms. Carol's niece."

I swallowed.

A knowing grin crossed Rikki's face, and her tongue made a ticking sound.

I put my hand back on my hip. "*What* are you talking about?"

"Mama said that Ms. Carol's niece *likes* Uncle Ray. Like maybe even as a boyfriend. And Mama thinks Uncle Ray likes her back, too."

"What do you mean 'likes her back'? That's ridiculous." I figured that Rikki was only trying to get back at me for inviting Golden to Darwin's pool party, but I still wanted to hear what she had to say. And boy, was she anxious to tell it.

"Mama said that Uncle Ray thinks Ms. Carol's niece is real pretty."

Well. So what? I've heard Daddy say that a lot of women were beautiful. "And?" I said.

"And"—Rikki took a deep breath and took her hand off the door—"she said that Uncle Ray hadn't had this much fun in a long time."

"Yeah right. Daddy has fun all the time."

"She works for an airline or something like that," Rikki continued.

"Oh, wait. And let me guess. I'm not supposed to know about this, either? Don't say anything to Daddy, right? Just like what you *thought* you heard about Daddy making me go to private school."

She shrugged. "Go on ahead and tell. I'll just deny it if Uncle Ray asks me if I said it. See if I care. And I *did* hear Mama say that Uncle Ray was thinking about sending you to Clara Ellis."

I cleared my throat and reminded her, "Only you didn't say 'thinking about.' You said he definitely was."

"Same thing."

"Whatever, Rikki." I pulled open the door and marched inside so that I could get away from her.

But maybe it wasn't really Rikki that I was angry with. Why in the *world* was Daddy keeping so many secrets from me?

Following close behind me, Rikki tried to sound reassuring. "Uncle Ray is probably gonna tell you, Cassidy. He probably just doesn't want you to be mad. You know, with the divorce and all."

I bit down real hard on my tongue, so hard that afterward I was surprised I didn't taste any blood.

"She's probably ugly," Rikki suggested.

"Who cares if she is?" I snapped. "My mother is beautiful too, even more so, and she'll be back in a year."

"Ten months," Rikki happily corrected me, trying to sound cheerful. "So this woman had better be ready to run."

"The only reason Daddy likes listening to the blues is because he misses Mom and can't wait for her to come back from Africa." I didn't really know if that was true, but I thought it could be.

"Ms. Carol's niece is probably desperate. Probably looking for a husband real bad like those women in church Mama's always talking about."

Who did this woman think she was? Didn't she know how busy Daddy was running his own business? Did she honestly think he really had time to date? He had me, plus work, *plus* cutting the grass to worry about. And didn't she know that divorce doesn't have to mean forever?

Rikki was smiling now. "Ms. Carol is a *sharrrp* old woman, don't get me wrong. I like the way her heels always match her purse and everything, how she be wearing them bad hats, the kind like I'm gonna wear one day. Watch. But, I still bet that niece of hers is butt ugly. She's probably *oogly*. I bet she wears corduroys and frumpy sweatshirts."

I chuckled. "Yeah. And I bet her teeth are yellow," I said as I began looking at the candy selection. The corner store is small and dusty, and sometimes the Now and Laters are abnormally hard. Trial and error has taught us what not to purchase.

"I bet her breath stinks," Rikki whispered.

"I bet she can't dance," I whispered back as I walked toward the end of the aisle.

"I bet she's dumb." Rikki followed close beside me.

We both laughed. "Oh, I *know* she's dumb," I said.

"And if she doesn't go away on her own, Cassidy, we'll just have to *make* her."

"How?"

"I don't know. We'll think of something, I'm sure, if we have to." Rikki picked up a box of Boston Baked Beans and a pack of Juicy Fruit. "Because I don't know who she thinks she is, coming around here trying to marry my uncle Ray."

I grabbed a pack of Starburst and some Skittles. "I know," I said.

"With her old ugly self."

"Oogly," I said. "Remember?"

Rikki laughed. "Right. Well, you know what I meant."

There was no air conditioner in the store, and the fan behind the counter was blowing out warm air. Mr. Post was behind the counter grinning, and his face was shining with sweat. He had big, round wet spots in the armpits of his T-shirt.

"Well look-a here," he chuckled. "The *Carter* girls! How's your daddy?" he said to me.

"Fine, thanks," I replied as I slid open the glass door to the soda case. I grabbed a Sprite for me and a Cherry Coke for Rikki.

"Lookin' more and more like your daddy every time I see you, I do declare. Jet-black hair, just like him. You know your daddy and me used to play peewee ball together when we were kids, back in the day. Just round the corner from here, 'bout three, four blocks over, matter fact. We used to call him Tonto, looked so much like one of them Indians."

I handed him my money. "Yeah, I know." I sighed at the same politically incorrect history lesson that he gives me all the time.

"Mr. Big Shot." He grinned. "See him all the time now, 'round the city, ridin' around in his Cat-lack. Mr. Computer Man. Mr. Busy Man. Tell your old man I said, 'Hey.' Old jive turkey. Tell him I remember when he used to drive a scooter, them little knobby knees out delivering newspapers."

"Will do, Mr. Post," I replied.

"Yeah . . . So, what ya'll doing for Labor Day?" He wanted to know. "Barbecuing?"

"I don't know. Maybe."

He looked at Rikki. "Your daddy still preachin'?"

"Ain't nothing changed since the last time you asked me." Rikki rolled her eyes. "And I already know—tell my daddy you said, 'Hey, jive turkey.'" She tapped her fingers on the counter.

"I swear, if you don't act just like your mama," he said. "Back in the day, ooh-wee."

Rikki held out her hand and waited. "My change, please?"

Mr. Post chuckled as he counted out the coins. "Yeah, them Carter boys always did get all the fine girls."

I braced myself, knowing what was coming.

He said, "Heard from that mama of yours? Out somewhere in the jungle, ain't she? That's what I hear. We'll have to call her Jane."

Rikki snatched my bag off the counter and thrust it at me. "Let's go," she said.

"'Bye, Mr. Post," I called back as we left the store.

Once we were outside Rikki tugged at my arm, mimicking Mr. Post's chuckle. "'Your daddy and me used to play peewee ball together.'" She doubled over laughing. "'Your mama sure was fine.' What does he want, a cookie, every time we have to hear that?"

I laughed with her. "I know."

"He's so gross. I swear it."

"And stupid."

"And everybody knows," she said as she crunched on a few Boston Baked Beans, "that our daddies are still the best. Talking all that 'back in the day' stuff. That's why Ms. Carol's niece is chasing Uncle Ray. Chickenhead. That's all she is, is a cluck."

That stopped me.

Wow. Could Daddy actually have a girlfriend?

"Rikki?"

"What's up?"

"Uh . . ."

Recognizing the quiver in my voice, she said, "Bite down on your tongue, Cassidy."

But I didn't want to. Maybe if a tear came out, if I let it fall, I'd feel better. Without crying, I managed to ask, "Do you really think Daddy is seeing Ms. Carol's niece?"

Rikki hesitated. "Well . . ."

"Because that just wouldn't be right. So soon, you know? Don't you think?"

Rikki nodded. "See? That's why we've got to keep things in the family the same. That's why we can't let anybody infiltrate."

"What do you mean?"

"Like invade on our territory," Rikki explained. "That's what Mary said about Tonya Randles liking Archie, that she'd better not try to infiltrate."

"Oh," I said. But I had the distinct feeling Rikki wasn't only talking about Ms. Carol's chickenhead niece doing the infiltrating.

August 25

Dear Mom,

I know I haven't written in my journal lately. It's not that I haven't wanted to, just so you know. I've been pretty busy, that's all.

I'm sure you're pretty busy too. I'm sure that's why you haven't called in a few days. I know you said it's not always convenient with the time difference and all. The phone rang real late the other night and I thought it was you that Daddy was talking to, but it wasn't. Maybe it was one of the guys from the band. Not that they have much to talk about, I'm sure. You know, maybe he just wanted to say hello or something.

eleven

The following Saturday I told Daddy that Mary was going to pick us all up from Golden's house on her way to work and drop us off at the movies. Afterward we would go to Gino's Pizza. It was actually becoming fun, keeping secrets from Daddy for a change.

Rikki, of course, told Uncle Lance and Aunt Honey the same thing, and they agreed to let Golden stay the night, stressing that they expected us back home as soon as Mary got off work.

So the plan was set.

Golden did my hair in crimps, and Rikki wore hers down too, more full and curly, though. Rikki said that if Golden was going to come with us, she had to let Rikki do something with her hair. So Rikki had brushed it up into a real high ponytail like *I Dream of Jeanie* and, for the first time, I realized how lovely Golden's eyes are. They're a butterscotch-tinted shade of hazel.

Golden hadn't told her mother anything about where we were going. Not the truth, not even a lie. In fact, when Mrs. Anders cheerfully asked where we were going to hang out for the day, Golden had clenched her teeth together and groaned.

"I'm sorry, honey," Mrs. Anders had said. "Too pushy?"

"Way," Golden replied.

I could tell by the smile in Rikki's eyes that she was impressed. As we finished primping in the bathroom, Rikki asked Golden how she managed to keep her mother in check like that.

"What do you mean?" Golden asked.

"She doesn't even *care* where you're going?" Rikki asked.

"She saw me with my swimsuit," Golden said. "I mean, come on. She'll say anything to make me talk to her. All because a guy comes by in his big blue van and tells us that we need to communicate more."

I'd seen that man the other day. Long silver hair in a ponytail, wearing khaki shorts, Birkenstocks, and a white T-shirt. I asked Golden if that was her mother's boyfriend or something, and it was the first time I heard her laugh.

"Yeah, right," she said. "Please. That's Mr. Burns. Our headman."

I didn't know what a headman was, and I wasn't sure if I should ask. Rikki was eyeing me suspiciously, with an I-told-you-so look on her face.

Hadn't I prayed for normal neighbors? The Anderses might turn out to be even worse than the Thompsons. Would a headman be scarier than a mortician?

"What in the *world*," Rikki asked Golden, "is a headman?"

Golden didn't answer at first, and I thought that maybe she was dismissing the question with silence.

"He's a shrink," she finally said. "My mom makes Freddy and me talk to him about the divorces and stuff because she thinks we can't handle it all on our own. Like we're still babies or something. It's so stupid, though. If anyone can't handle things, it's her. I hate talking to him. He's gross."

Rikki started shaking her head, and I took a deep breath and swallowed. How many times had Golden's mom been married?

Golden thought some more. "He makes me *sick*," she added. "He thinks he knows so much, I swear."

Without saying a word, Rikki just kept shaking her head back and forth. There was something very secretive about Golden, but now she was opening up to us a little. I didn't want to risk annoying her by asking too many questions, though, so I decided to just let the subject drop. Golden could tell us more whenever she was ready. Besides, I didn't want whatever Golden had to say to give Rikki a dozen more reasons why we shouldn't be friends with her.

We could hear Mrs. Anders coming up the hallway, and she stopped in the doorway of the bathroom with her big

Nikon camera. Again.

"*Mom*," Golden said, "isn't that the whole roll yet?"

Mrs. Anders was smiling from behind the lens as she snapped yet another picture. "Nope," she said, and snapped again. "How about a group one, girls?"

We pressed our faces together and smiled as Mrs. Anders snapped away some more.

"Okay, Mom," Golden said. "Enough."

But Mrs. Anders giggled, and snapped one last candid picture before she left us alone.

Golden got out huge pink towels from the linen closet for us to use as wraparounds. We helped one another put them on and tie them up in big fat knots at our sides.

Usually at pool parties I wear my jean shorts over my suit and just put my feet in the water. I'd never worn a swimming suit in front of a boy before, and I was having second thoughts. But I looked in the mirror and saw Rikki's and Golden's faces reflected back at me, their approving smiles, and I reconsidered. Everyone was so excited. I couldn't back out now. And, hey, maybe Darwin's pool party would even turn out to be fun.

"You look awesome, Cass," Golden assured me.

"Yeah, *Cassidy*." Rikki rolled her eyes a bit. She was still refusing to use my new nickname. "You do."

"And so do you, Golden," I added.

"Well, I think we *all* look good," Rikki declared.

Just before we left the bathroom, Golden yanked open the

drawer under the sink, fumbled around, and grabbed a few tubes of lip gloss, all pretty shades of pink.

"Girls," Mrs. Anders yelled, "Mary's here!"

"We'll put it on in the car," Golden said as we headed downstairs.

Mary had wanted us to make a big entrance, so we got to Darwin's late. When we pulled up, she told us, "Now remember, I get off at eight, so I'll pick you up at the corner at eight-thirty."

"Okay," we all said.

Mary smiled. "You girls look so adorable. Have fun."

We could smell the barbecue, hear the laughter, and feel the bass from the blaring stereo as soon as we got out of the car. The closer we got to the fence, the louder the music became. A cardboard sign was hanging on the gate with bright red graffiti letters: PARTY OF THE SUMMER HERE.

As soon as we walked through the gate we saw Mr. and Mrs. Mack, Darwin's parents. Mr. Mack was wearing a black and gold apron with "BBQ King" on the front, and Mrs. Mack was carrying a stack of paper plates over to a table.

"Glad you could make it," Mr. Mack said.

"Plenty of food," Mrs. Mack added with a smile. "Hot dogs. Potato salad. Brats. Burgers. It's all over on the table, so go on. Enjoy."

"Okay." Rikki sounded all sweet and innocent. "We will, Mrs. Mack."

Everyone watched us walk through the yard. Or maybe not. Maybe it just seemed like it. Maybe it always feels like people are watching me and they aren't. I tried real hard to make my nervousness disappear.

The Macks' backyard is huge. Some kids were in the pool, but others were scattered throughout the yard, sitting on lawn chairs or at picnic tables. Quite a few were dancing up on the wooden deck. Several people were just leaning up against the fence, cooling out and chitchatting with canned sodas in their hands. Rikki spotted some lawn chairs that were outside of splashing distance and suggested we grab them.

I looked back at the gate. What if Uncle Lance or Aunt Honey had followed us? What would they think? What would they do to the three of us, half naked in front of adolescent boys?

"Yo, Rikki!" Darwin's voice called out from the makeshift dance floor. He had been doing that new hustle, the Forrest Hills Flow, but he had stopped midstep to throw his hands in the air. "What up?" he yelled.

Rikki nudged me and couldn't help smiling. "Let me go dance with him real quick. Be right back, okay?

"Or," she added cautiously, "ya'll can come if you want."

I looked at Golden, who was looking around at the backyard full of kids. "That's okay. We're cool."

I filled Golden in on the history between Rikki and Darwin as Rikki walked away. "They always try to act like they don't like each other, but they can't be in a room together five minutes without getting close. Been that way since the beginning of sixth grade."

Golden got a good look at Darwin and said, "He's hot."

"You must like pretty boys," I joked. "But Darwin's nice. You'll see when you meet him later."

As I looked around the backyard full of familiar faces, I gave Golden the lowdown on who was going with who, who used to go with who, and who *she* should never go with.

"Who's *that*?" she asked with a raised eyebrow. "He's hot too."

I followed her gaze. Splashing around in the pool, squirting a water gun at anyone within aiming distance, was Travis.

"Oh," I said. "That's just Travis Jones."

"*Really*?" Golden stared a little longer. "As in *the* Travis?" Rikki had filled her in on my hatred of Travis on the car ride over.

"He's gotten better looking over the summer, trust me."

"You're not gonna believe this," Golden said. "But I've seen him before. Somewhere . . . I don't know. . . ."

"He was in California all summer," I said, "so I doubt it."

"Hmmm." She crossed one leg over the other. "Maybe not."

"Like I said, he's gotten *a lot* better. He discovered lotion, got taller, darker, braces. . . ."

"Well, he looks better than some of the woofs I used to know at my old school."

"You ever go with anybody?"

"Not at my last school," Golden said. "But at the school before that I did. I kissed this lame-o named Jeff last year, but that was about it. I think I was bored or something."

Great. I was officially the last girl in the entire world who had yet to be kissed.

Golden looked around some more. "So who do you like?"

"Yeah, right."

"Not even a little bit? Nobody?"

I shrugged. "They're all just annoying."

"Hey," she asked, "what about those three, over there by the fence."

"Nate is on the left. Mario is the one with the glasses; you have to watch him, though, because he likes to crack on people. The skinny one is Sam. Sam's cool. All of 'em hoop."

"Does Travis?"

"Yeah," I said. "But he usually sits the bench."

Travis looked up from the pool then, like he sensed that we were talking about him, and nodded his head up.

"S'up?" he called.

I mumbled to Golden, "I can't stand him."

"You could at least say 'Hi,'" she suggested. "Since he did."

So Golden and I both waved.

Why, oh why, did we do that? Travis climbed up the ladder, got out of the pool, and came right on over. Before I knew it, Travis was standing in front of me, his green shorts dripping water everywhere. Inside I was cringing.

"What's up?" he asked. "Thought you weren't coming."

"Changed my mind," I said.

His braces sparkled when he smiled. "Tight suit."

"Thanks." I folded my arms across my chest.

Glancing back at the pool, he said, "Comin' in?"

"Maybe later."

He noticed Golden. "Who's your friend?"

"She's new," I said, "so be nice. Her name is Golden Anders. Golden, meet Travis Jones."

"Straight up?" Travis said. "Where you from?"

"Around," Golden replied. "I used to go to Lake. And my last name is Mahoney, not Anders."

Instantly I wanted to apologize. I hadn't even considered that Golden would have a different name from her mother's. Then I heard the surprise in Travis's voice. "Yo! You went to Lake? When?"

"Last year."

"For real? So you know my cousin then, huh? Tony?"

"Tony Jones?"

"For sure."

"Yeah," Golden said. "I know Tony. He's cool."

"So you comin' to King now? Our team is gonna run it," Travis told her. "Bet."

"Cool," she said.

And then Travis looked at me. "You eat yet?"

"No."

"Hungry?"

"No."

He raised an eyebrow. "Thirsty?"

"No." I kinda laughed. "I'm cool."

"What? You still mad at me? You want me to leave?"

"I'm not mad," I said. But I really did want him to leave.

"Then why you throw my ice cream away?" Travis asked. "If you weren't mad?"

Golden cracked up laughing, which made me do the same.

Travis laughed a little too. "It's cool," he said. He glanced at me as he headed back to the pool. "You gonna dance with me later, though, right?"

My stomach got tight and my teeth clenched.

Why did that keep happening?

I shrugged.

"All right then," he said. "But I'm gone get you in that pool."

Travis smiled, and a flutter shot through my stomach and went up through my chest. I watched as he dove back into the water and started splashing around again.

I told Golden, "*Now* do you see how annoying he is?"

"I *knew* I'd seen him before," she said, ignoring my question. "He used to come hang in my old neighborhood with Tony and his crew."

"Really?"

"Yeah," she said. "I remember him because this girl named Keisha used to really like him."

"And what happened?"

"She was kinda dorky, and I hear he's real picky. His

cousin Tony is too."

I watched Travis as he flicked water in girls' faces.

"Travis?" I said. "Picky? Really?"

"Uh-huh," Golden said. "Selective. And you're right, he did get taller."

Come to think of it, I couldn't recall Travis ever really liking a whole lot of girls. He teased *all* of us, but who had he ever really *liked*?

Erica Turner in the fourth grade, but that was about it, and she moved to Philadelphia last year.

"It sure is hot," Golden said. "Let's go get in."

Panic hit my chest, and I gripped the knot on my towel. "The pool, you mean?"

"We might as well," Golden said. "Since we're here."

I was *so* glad Golden was with me. There was no way I'd have moved from my seat if she weren't. We left our towels on the chair and headed over to the pool.

We decided to just sit on the edge at first, to let our feet get used to the temperature for a while. We didn't talk much. It was so hot that all we really had the strength to do was sit there and take it. The water on our feet hinted at relief, and I knew that eventually Golden would want to get in, and I was dreading that.

All around us were people that I had gone to school with for years, which wasn't surprising. If Darwin throws a party, *everyone* wants to be there. There was one person missing that I could see, but just then she arrived.

twelve

Lane Benson. The first girl in our class to stop wearing ponytails. The first to get a training bra (the first to actually have something to train). The first to wear makeup (if you count eyeliner and lip gloss). The first to be allowed to have phone calls from boys. And talk about an entrance. Now Lane Benson was also the first of us to wear a bikini. A black one.

From across the yard, Rikki's eyes met mine, both of us in shock. A hush fell throughout the yard, and I could see people tapping each other. Boys smiling. Girls whispering. I was ready to leave.

Golden leaned in. "Let me guess. Lane Benson?"

I sighed. "You got it."

"She tries too hard," Golden announced. "You're prettier, Cass."

Shantal and the rest of the training bra crew went right over to Lane and led her back to the picnic table where they'd been sitting. Lane smiled when she saw them, her dimples like valleys in her round, dark-brown cheeks.

Then she saw me looking at her, which meant it was too late for me to turn away. We exchanged words with our eyes. It was like she wanted me to know that my very presence disgusted her, the way she mocked me with a flutter of her eyelashes. Right then and there I promised myself not to let her ruin this day for me. Hopefully my eyes did what I needed them to do, because I sure tried to look happy.

Soon the moment passed, and people got over the fact that Lane had arrived in a bikini. The water began splashing around us again, and Travis started up a game of Marco Polo.

Golden hopped into the water. "Come on, Cass!"

I was now the only one left on the edge of the pool. Everyone else was having fun. Reluctantly, I lowered myself in.

"Whatever you do," Golden whispered a quick warning, "make sure Lane sees you having fun."

"I know," I said. "That's just what I was thinking too."

I peeked over once more. Lane was sitting at a round table with her small group of girls. She was eating a hot dog, laughing and talking in between bites. Yuck. Boy, was I glad that I wasn't going to have to go to school with her anymore.

But at least now I wasn't alone. I had Golden, and she was forcing me to have fun. She herself looked to be having a good time, which made me even happier because I had a feeling that didn't happen too often. Pretty soon I forgot all about Lane.

Rikki and Darwin joined us in the pool. More laughter. More games. Rikki was even being a little nicer to Golden, reaching up once to fix a few strands on Golden's ponytail as a matter of fact. It was the best day of summer, and it felt great to laugh out loud. None of us wanted the games to end.

All the hot dogs had been grilled and the sun was beginning to set. Darwin's parents cooled off the coals and went inside to the air-conditioning. By now most of us had thrown on jean shorts over our swimming suits. Soon it would be the last song of the evening.

Rikki was with Darwin, and Golden and I were sitting on the steps leading to the deck, watching as couples started going off to be alone.

"All of your friends are so cool, Cass," Golden said. "Thanks for inviting me."

"Sure," I replied.

We watched as Lane and Nate went to the far end of the backyard and sat on the wooden swing. Shantal and Mario were getting close at the picnic table. Everyone was coupling off except for Whitney and a few other girls who were on the dance floor doing a routine they'd probably been practicing for weeks. My heart sank when Sam came over to Golden with his hand out.

"Wanna dance?" he said.

It didn't seem to make Golden nervous at all, to reach out and put her hand in his. "Be right back," she told me. And together they walked up the steps to the deck.

And there I sat, alone.

Travis was wearing a green and white Nike T-shirt and a grin on his face as he walked over to me. "You wanna dance?" he asked politely.

The tightness in my stomach was back. "No," I replied.

Travis put one foot on the step where I was sitting and listened to the music for a few seconds. With a smile in his eyes, he shrugged. "Not even on a good song?"

I wanted him to leave, to go find somebody else to annoy, but he sat down next to me, *real close*, so close that I could feel his leg against mine. More flutters in my stomach, and even in my *chest* this time. My teeth started chattering.

I was cold, that was all.

"Your hair looks tight," he said.

"Thanks," I replied. "Golden did it."

"She seems cool."

"She is."

Travis seemed to be waiting for me to look at him, so I did. "What?"

He just kept smiling, looking like he was going to laugh.

"What?" I said again.

"Why you always actin' so mean, Cassidy?"

I looked away. "I'm not."

"And why are you diggin' your nails into your arm like that?"

I looked down. Travis was right. I relaxed and rested my

hands in my lap. But I definitely still had those flutters.

"Your nails look pretty too," he told me.

"Thanks," I said. "My cousin Mary painted them to match my suit."

"For real? I know Mary. She's cool with my sister."

"I know," I said. "Sharee, right?"

"Yeah . . ."

And then there was more silence. Endless and forever silence. I wanted to get up and run out of the backyard, but where would I go? Silence. Silence. Too much silence.

Finally Travis said, "For real. You know how I like you, right?"

Oh my goodness! I could hardly hear for the pounding in my ears. What in the world was I supposed to say to that?

I couldn't believe it, but Travis's face showed no signs of kidding.

"This year I might get to start. You could come to all my games, sit with my moms and pops up in the stands and everything."

"You're always playing around, Travis," I said.

"Straight up," he said, sounding really sincere. "You should be my lady, Cassidy."

I remembered that day at the park when Darwin had asked Rikki to go off with him so that Travis could be alone with me. Was Travis really being honest? I could sense him looking at me again, and I tried hard to keep looking right back.

"What?" I said.

He cracked a smile and nudged me. "Mean."

"I'm not."

"Yes, you are."

"No," I said. "And as a matter of fact, I'm also not stuck-up. Since you guys made everybody think that I am, let's get that straight right now. I'm a very nice person. Golden moved in next door to me and I was nice to her. You're the one who's mean, Travis. Let's talk about who made me drop my goldfish and then laughed when I did."

Travis was speechless.

I continued, "So, maybe I don't always want to talk to you because maybe you haven't always been so nice to me, Travis. Ever thought about *that*?"

Wow. It sure felt good to speak my mind for a change.

After a moment he said, "Well, we really were just playin'."

"Well, it wasn't much fun."

"I tried to catch up with you to tell you, but you—"

"And *you* laughed the loudest," I pointed out to him.

"Look. It's not because I didn't like you, all right? Like I said, we were just—"

"You could've just come over and said, 'Hi,' Travis." I was on a roll now. "How about that? If you like somebody and want to be friends, sometimes you can just go over to them and say, 'Hi.' You could have asked me about my fish, what his name was going to be."

He looked a little uncomfortable. “Can we just forget about that day, pretend it never happened?”

“No.”

“Why not?”

“Because it did, Travis.”

He sighed. “Well, all I can say is that I’m sorry then. Dang.”

I felt my face start to cool off. “Well, that’s a start.”

“Let’s just go for a walk.”

“No.”

“Why?”

“Because I don’t wanna leave.”

“I’m just talking about away from the speakers and everybody.” He stood up and waited.

I shook my head. “No thanks.”

“Man, Cassidy, come on. Stop trippin’.” He held his hand out for me to hold. “Come on. For real.”

I stared at his hand, waiting for *me* to hold, and my heart fluttered, *hard* this time.

Rikki and Darwin. Golden and Sam. Mary and Archie.

Me and Travis?

“Cassidy,” he said. “Come on.”

But what else were we going to talk about? I’d already said all the things that I’d ever wanted to say to Travis.

“Fine,” I replied. And my heart rippled again.

thirteen

Travis looked like he couldn't believe what he'd just heard. He was even *more* shocked when I reached out and put my hand in his. He squeezed it tight, like he wanted to make sure it was really there, but then he relaxed, which made me do the same.

After we started walking, he said, "You cold?"

Actually, I was only shivering because I was nervous, but I didn't admit that. "No," I said. "I'm okay."

As we walked past the shed I caught a glimpse of Rikki, her arms reaching up, wrapped snug around Darwin's neck, his hands on her butt, right there in plain view. Uncle Lance and Aunt Honey would have had a fit!

Suddenly I planted my feet right there in the grass. Travis better not try to touch my butt.

Travis looked confused. "What?"

"Nothing." I shook my head. No matter what, there was no way I was going to let that happen. No. Way.

Once we were around the side of the house, Travis leaned up against the house and took my other hand in his. I felt my face burning again as I saw both of our hands together.

He asked, "Will you wear your hair like that to my games?"

I looked away. To his games? Was he serious? He was really serious. This was really happening. He gave my hands a squeeze and laughed. "What? You don't think I'm cute?" he said jokingly.

I couldn't help but laugh a little too.

He laughed some more. "What? My breath stinks? I got bad BO?"

I laughed a little louder now. Laughing sure does help when you're nervous.

And then Travis was quiet for a minute. "For real, Cassidy. My bad about your fish."

I started to pull my hands out of his, but he felt me doing so and gripped them tighter.

"Do you forgive me?" he wanted to know.

I shrugged.

And then I wondered, why *didn't* I like Travis? He wasn't anywhere near as silly as he used to be, he was much cuter now, and he did seem genuinely apologetic about what happened to Goldie.

He asked me, "When is your birthday?"

"October."

"October what?"

"Twenty-third."

"All right," he said. "And what's your favorite color?"

I sighed. "Purple. Why?"

"You like Starburst, Skittles, or Snickers?"

"I don't know. Why?"

"For your birthday," he suggested. "How about I'll buy you a new fish, something purple, and some candy. Cool?"

That all sounded pretty nice, but wait a minute. If I said okay, did that mean I was his girlfriend? Just in case, I didn't say anything.

He asked, "What else?"

"Travis, look." I sighed.

"S'up?"

"You don't have to buy me another fish. That was never the point."

"Okay." He shrugged. "So now what?"

"Are you really serious?"

"T. Money don't play," he said.

I gave him a look. "Yeah. Right."

He laughed. "Well, not like I used to. On the real, though. On everything, you gonna let me get those seven, or what?"

I smacked my lips, reminding myself of Rikki. "I'm not even sure if I can *have* phone calls from boys." This was true. Daddy and I had never talked about it.

"Oh." He sounded disappointed.

"Well, I just need to ask my dad," I said.

His face brightened a bit, and he shrugged. "All right then. Cool. How 'bout I'll just give you mine?"

"I guess," I said.

"So what time you gonna call?"

"I don't know," I said. I couldn't believe it. Was I actually going to pick up the phone and *call* Travis Jones?

He thought for a minute. "Better call before ten. After that, you have to let the phone ring once, then call back five minutes later. I'll hurry up and call somebody and be on the other line so the phone won't ring. Cool?"

I was so nervous that my voice came out shaky. "All right."

He squinted his eyes. "So, do you think I'm cute?"

"Travis . . ." I managed to say through my giggles.

He put on a playful face, and kept waiting, and waiting.

I smiled. "I guess." I let the *s* sound linger for a moment. "But only now, since you're nicer."

"Come here," he said, trying to pull me closer.

But I plastered myself right where I was. "For what?" I asked.

"Just to chill," he said. "Come on."

I waited for a long time, so long that his smile dissolved and he started biting his bottom lip. "What? What's wrong now, Cassidy?"

I swallowed real hard, and I still couldn't move. Travis's eyes were so hopeful, and his hair was still glistening with pool water. He really did look harmless. *And* cute.

"Cassidy." He reached out and held my hand again. "I really do like you." Then, very gently, he pulled me toward him. This time, I let him.

With his face close to mine, he put his hand on my waist. I tried to reposition myself so that his arm would fall off me, but it didn't. He grabbed tighter, and I looked around. I really was all alone with Travis.

He said, "So, you coming to my games?"

Amid the flutters, I felt myself smiling inside, but I didn't answer. Was Travis going to be my very first boyfriend?

He raised his eyebrows. "You gonna come?"

I felt myself beaming, more comfortable now, and I was glad for that. "Maybe," I teased. I barely recognized myself. I was behaving like Rikki.

He feigned a sad expression. "*All right then.* Be like that. It's cool. . . ."

I nudged him with my shoulder. "Travis, I didn't say no," I reminded him.

A silly, dramatic wave of relief passed across his face, and then he grew quiet, more serious again. For a moment I could only hear low voices in the backyard as the music on the stereo changed from one song to a slower one.

After the music started again, Travis said, "You never kissed nobody before, have you?"

"I don't do stuff like that," I said.

He pulled me closer into him.

I pulled back a little. "Travis . . ."

He smiled. "What? I'm not talking about doing the *grown up*."

"Oh, I *really* don't do stuff like *that*."

He put his hand on the small of my back, but this time I didn't push it away. It actually felt okay.

"That's what I like about you," he said. "You're different."

"What do you mean?"

"All some girls talk about *is* doing the grown up."

"Really? Like who?"

"Like everybody." He shrugged.

"Well, not me."

"I know," he said. "That's why you're different."

And again, he pulled me into him. Just that quick, before I knew what was happening, before I even had a chance to take a deep breath first, Travis's mouth was on mine, and he was pressing in.

After a couple of seconds, he pulled away.

"Cassidy," he said. "You gotta kiss back."

He moved toward me again. This time, when his lips pressed against mine, I remembered to do what he'd said. We held still like that for a while, my heart bursting with all kinds of new and unfamiliar flutters, and it felt nice, *very* nice, as a matter of fact.

Finally he pulled his face from mine.

I had just kissed Travis Jones!

And now we were looking into each other's eyes.

More flutters.

He bit his bottom lip again.

I waited. What was wrong? Did I not do something that I was supposed to do? "What?" I said.

Travis smiled a little, then pulled me back toward him, pressing his lips against mine again. It was harder this time, more forceful. And something was different. Travis's mouth was opened. It was what Rikki had told me about, what she and Darwin did all the time. French kissing. Mary had always said that it would feel wonderful, but actually, it felt pretty weird.

Then I remembered what Rikki had told me once, that you're not supposed to think while you're kissing, that you're just supposed to do what you feel. Otherwise it won't feel as good. So I tried to shut my mind off.

Travis reached down to take my other hand. He placed that one on his shoulder and then let go. Now I was standing kind of how Rikki was with Darwin. Only Travis didn't try to put his hand on my butt, and boy, was I glad.

We kissed some more, a *lot* more, the whole time with my hand around Travis's neck. I could feel his heart pounding, and I wondered if he could feel mine, too.

I was kissing for the first time, and Mary was right in how she'd described it. It really did feel like swinging on the last day of summer, when you don't want it to end.

When we were finished, Travis had kind of a nervous look on his face, and I knew that I did too.

"Now what?" I asked.

He shrugged. "Answer my question."

"What question?"

"Will you be my lady?"

Now I bit *my* bottom lip. That was something that I still wasn't ready to answer.

He let out a long breath. "So you gonna call me tonight, or what?"

"I guess," I said.

"All right. Nine forty-five," he said. "Cool?"

"Okay."

"Cool," he said again.

I felt so weird, like I was still kissing, even. How long would it take before that feeling went away and I could feel normal again? What if Travis went back to being the old Travis again, but I couldn't erase the way it felt to kiss him? But then again, what if he didn't? What if we did become boyfriend and girlfriend? What if everything that changes stays changed forever?

fourteen

At eight-thirty, Mary wasn't waiting for us at the corner. Unfortunately, Aunt Honey was.

Rikki spotted the fog lights on her parents' big brown van first and immediately stopped walking. Golden and I, of course, followed suit.

"No use runnin'," Rikki said with a heavy sigh. "Damage is done now." She took a piece of gum out of her plastic bag of take-home goodies from the party, popped it in her mouth, and headed straight for the van.

Aunt Honey was by herself, sitting in the driver's seat shaking her head back and forth. She didn't say anything as the three of us piled in.

"But Ma—" Rikki started in.

"Not a word," Aunt Honey interrupted. "*Not* a word." Then she reached back and snatched Rikki's bag, peeked inside, snagged a roll of Smarties, and twisted the wrapper open. Piece by piece she crunched.

I looked over at Rikki, her face barely visible in the dark shadows in the back of the van. Golden's eyes were huge, like she didn't know what in the world was about to happen. She didn't know Aunt Honey.

"Big ole loud bark," Rikki whispered to Golden, "no bite. Watch."

But, then again, we'd never been caught like this before. Coming out of a party with swimming suits on? What *was* going to happen to Rikki? And what would happen to *me*?

"Cassidy," Aunt Honey said, "your father is on his way to our house to get you and Golden. He's very, very upset with you."

I sighed. "Okay."

"Okay, Mrs. Carter," Golden said too.

We were pulling into the driveway before Aunt Honey spoke again. "There is no way in our Father's world that I'd have ever imagined my daughters *and* my niece would lie to me," she said. "Lord have mercy."

I noticed that Mary's car was parked in the garage with the windows rolled up all the way and not on the street like it usually is. Rikki asked, "Where is she?"

Aunt Honey said, "The question is, where was she when she was *supposed* to be at work?"

Rikki stormed down the stairs into the basement where Golden and I sat frozen in silence on the couch. She had been upstairs talking, or rather yelling, with Aunt Honey and Uncle Lance for a while, and now she was muttering that she was going to run away.

Uncle Lance marched down the steps after Rikki, which was surprising. Uncle Lance and Aunt Honey hardly ever come downstairs. "Don't you storm through my house like this," Uncle Lance fumed.

Rikki rolled her eyes and flopped down beside me on the couch. With her arms crossed, she started tapping her foot.

Uncle Lance stood in front of us and looked at me. Then he looked at Golden. His eyes went from bulging with anger to nervous confusion as he started pacing back and forth.

"Look. I am your father," he reminded Rikki, as if she didn't know this. "And you *will* respect me." His nostrils flared as he shook his pointer finger in the air.

"But Daddy, you just don't—"

"No!" He cut her off. "You will honor me in my house. And as long as you are *my* child, you will obey me. Until you learn to do as you're told, until you learn that deceit is a sin, you will be punished. Do you hear me?"

"Can I just say something, Daddy? Please? Can I at least tell you something?"

"You lied to me. You lied to your mother. There will be no forked tongues in my house, little girl."

"But Daddy! All I'm trying to tell you is that all the other kids were there." Rikki's voice cracked, which made me look at her. Just then a tear fell. Whoa. Rikki never cries.

I wanted to tell her to bite her tongue, the way she always tells me, but I was too nervous that Uncle Lance would start yelling at me, too, so I just touched her shoulder instead.

Rikki sniffed. "Daddy, here it is, big ole summer, and I couldn't even go over to my friend's party? All we ever get to do is go to church. Wouldn't God want me to have fun?"

Uncle Lance looked at me. "Cassidy, what did your father say?"

Rikki spoke before I had a chance to answer. "She hasn't talked to him yet. But he'll probably understand, Daddy. See, Uncle Ray is normal!"

Uncle Lance frowned. "Now look here—"

"Daddy . . ." Rikki whined. "It's not like Darwin's parents weren't there—"

"W-w-what did you say?" he stuttered. "That makes lying to your mother and me right? The fact that the Macks were home? The sin I am addressing is deceit. Thou shall not lie, Rikki!"

Uncle Lance's eyes narrowed. "I have rules and regulations and you will abide by them. Two months. I'm sure your mother will want to add something to—"

Rikki jumped up off the couch. "Two months of what?"

"You will not leave this house for the next two months. School and church, that's it. That'll give you plenty of time to think about how a responsible young lady conducts herself." Uncle Lance's voice faded into mumbling as he turned and made his way upstairs.

No longer fighting back her tears, Rikki insisted that she was coming to live with me.

A few minutes later, Mary crept downstairs.

"Hey," she whispered as she sat down cautiously on the La-Z-Boy, as if extra noise would make things worse. As if anything could make things worse. Mary's eyes were red and puffy like she'd been doing an awful lot of crying herself. I couldn't remember ever being angry with Mary, but I guess there is a first time for everything.

"What do *you* want?" Rikki asked, just what I was thinking.

"Rikki, girls, look," Mary said, taking care to look at each of us. "I'm sorry."

"What happened?" I asked.

Mary sighed. "It was so embarrassing. I thought that maybe it was one of you calling when my cell phone rang, otherwise I never would have answered. Of all the days for Daddy to come by the DQ to check on me . . . I wasn't there, so he called my cell phone."

"But you were *supposed* to be there," I reminded her.

"I know, I know," she said. "But Archie wanted to see me, so I got someone to cover for me while I left for a little bit."

"So what," Rikki said. "Daddy called so you decided to play us by telling him where we were? Whatever, Mary."

"He threatened to take my car, Rikki! To make me quit my job. My only two ways of getting out of this house were going to be gone for months! And you know Daddy never backs down once he issues a punishment. He *demanded* to know where you were. It was awful."

"Well, still, it's your fault for leaving work," Rikki said. "If you would've just followed the plan, none of this would've happened."

Rikki was right. Maybe Mary wasn't as smart as I always believed she was. I felt bad for thinking it, but Mary really did get flighty when it came to Archie. Rikki always says that whenever Archie comes around, Mary's brain grows wings and flies south and doesn't come back until he leaves.

Rikki started holding her breath, like she often does when she gets angry. She says that one day she is going to hold it until she dies. Golden laughed when I told her what Rikki was doing.

"Rikki," Mary said, "you know that eventually your brain takes over and *makes* you exhale. It's the body's autopilot for survival."

Still, Rikki's eyes were staring at the ceiling, tears falling steadily down her cheeks in dramatic punctuation.

Mary nodded with understanding. "I know just how you feel," she said. Then she reached over and pinched Rikki's stomach. Rikki pretended to be angry, but I could tell that she was relieved to breathe again.

"Dang, Mary," Rikki said. "You ruined everything."

"Trust me," Mary said, ignoring Rikki's anger. "I never would've left work if I thought any of this was going to happen."

Rikki wouldn't let up. "You're so stupid, I swear. Stupid. Stupid. Stupid. Leave it to stupid, stupid Mary."

Mary said, "Well, just be glad you got away with the pool party, okay? At least Mom didn't come in and embarrass you."

Rikki rolled her eyes and threw one of the couch pillows across the room. "I'm on punishment *again.* Darwin's birthday is coming, he's having a party, and I'll be the only person in the world who won't be able to go."

Mary walked over and picked up the pillow. "Well, you shouldn't be available all the time anyhow, Rikki. None of you should. Only common girls go to every event. Be selective. Your presence should be a compliment to the host."

Rikki whipped around and glared. "You're the stupidest person I've ever known! Shut up talking to me."

The anger I felt a minute before vanished, I felt so bad for Mary now. She had bought us those swimming suits and really had wanted us to have fun. No way she would have willingly ratted on us. Uncle Lance and Aunt Honey must've really put on the pressure. I probably would've cracked too.

But Mary was used to Rikki, so she just ignored her and looked over at Golden and me. A softness appeared in her eyes. "Did you two have fun at least?" she asked.

"I did," Golden said.

"Me too," I added.

Mary sang teasingly, *"Did you see Sharee's little brother?"*

I was so embarrassed that my face started burning.

Rikki hit me with another couch pillow. "Yeah, I saw ya'll go off on the side of the house too. What happened?"

Mary and Golden gasped.

"Cass!" Golden said.

Mary whispered, "Did you let him kiss you?"

"She did!" Rikki shrieked, satisfaction in her voice. "Look how she's smiling."

I really didn't want to think about Travis right now. I had enough things to fill up my brain. Being in trouble is stressful. But I couldn't lie. Just the mention of Travis's name made me remember our kiss. I felt a nice tingle inside.

Mary clasped her hands over her mouth and her eyes started watering. "Your first kiss! Oh, *Cassidy* . . ."

Golden looked shocked. "Really? Your first?"

"Bet he can't kiss," Rikki said. "He's got those stupid braces now. I bet his breath stunk."

"Ignore her," Mary said. She was still able to put up with Rikki, but it was getting harder and harder for me.

Rikki was the one who'd wanted me to give Travis a chance in the first place. Now that she was in trouble she was saying mean things about him? I swear. Sometimes. If Rikki wasn't my cousin . . .

Mary said, "So? Do you like him now?"

I shrugged. "I don't know. He's nicer now. So maybe. Well, a little bit."

"How adorable," Mary said.

I showed Mary and Golden the piece of paper I had in my pocket. The ink had smeared, but Travis's phone number was still readable.

“Oh.” Mary clutched her hand to her chest. “How sweet.”

Rikki fell back on the couch. “Call him. Tell him to tell Darwin how much I love him. I’ll probably never get to see him again.”

“You’ll see him again,” Mary assured Rikki. “Trust me. Mom and Dad are just upset right now. They’ll get over it.”

I heard the doorbell ring and I wondered, *but would Daddy?*

fifteen

"Cassidy Carter." Daddy was talking to me from the doorway of my bedroom, nowhere near as loud as Uncle Lance, but definitely just as upset. "I trusted you," he said.

The silence during the drive home had been better than those words. Way better.

I couldn't bear to look at him, so I stared a little to the left at my lava lamp instead.

"Look at me," Daddy said, and waited until I did. "Can you please explain all of this to me?"

"It was a pool party." I started with the facts. "A friend of ours from school invited us. His name is Darwin Mack, and he's really nice. I wanted Golden to meet some of the girls from school."

"But you *said* you were going to the movies and for pizza. You mentioned nothing about swimming."

What could I say?

He pulled out the chair from my desk, flipped it around, and sat on it with his hands tucked underneath his armpits. "I'm waiting," he said.

My voice was shaky, and I knew tears were close. "I was mad at you."

"At me? Why?"

"Because."

His tone shifted to being more firm. "Because *why* . . . ?"

"You were trying to send me to private school without even telling me," I started. "And now this thing with Ms. Carol's niece . . ."

Daddy looked completely shocked. "What in the world does this have to do with *Toni*? She's a good friend, but what has she got to do with any of this?"

"All she wants to do is get you to marry her so she can move into this big new house."

Daddy's mouth fell wide open. Then he got a cross look on his face. "Now that's enough," he said. "You are out of line. What has gotten into you? And who told you anything about Toni, anyhow?"

Realizing that Rikki would probably get punished even more for this, I kept my lips closed tight. Two months was already an eternity.

"Cassidy?"

"What difference does it make who told me? *You* didn't."

He let out a long breath. "Cassidy, I wish that I could

understand what it is that you're feeling right now, but I can't. Not if you don't tell me. I'm not a mind reader."

"You keep doing things without telling me."

He raised his chin, lifted his eyebrows, and then he flat-out looked tired.

"We wanted to talk to you when the letter came," he said. "But then Honey and Lance found out that Rikki's aptitude test scores were much lower than yours. We all decided that we didn't want Rikki to have to feel bad, so we never told either of you."

"Rikki's scores were too low to get into Clara Ellis?"

"Quite a bit," Daddy said. "And we thought it was best not to even bring it up. Honey said we should, that it wasn't fair to you, that you should still go, but I didn't agree. For months she's been encouraging me to send you there, you know, with the reputation of the school. But I just couldn't. Not with how close you and Rikki are. Not since your grades are already fine. Besides, the public schools need our support."

This all made sense to me. Rikki felt bad enough, having prison wardens for parents and all. Why make her feel stupid, too? It's funny. Just a couple of weeks ago, I was ready for some time away from Rikki, but now I felt bad for thinking that. Now I just wanted to see her and to let her know how glad I was that she's my cousin, but also my friend.

"And pumpkin, as far as Toni is concerned, your mother and I decided that until we're really sure that someone is going to be a major part of our lives, we aren't going to involve you. Things have been tough enough on you as it is."

"Oh" was all I could say.

He got up, kissed me on my forehead, and sighed, "But you lied to me, pumpkin. So for one week, no phone, no Rikki, no Golden. Understand?"

"Daddy!"

He raised an eyebrow. "Lance and Honey gave Rikki two *months*, didn't they?"

I sighed and nodded. I'm not stupid. One week sounded a whole lot better than two months, that's for sure.

Daddy closed the door behind him, but forgot to take my phone. For a while I alternated between eyeing the phone and the door. I kept listening to make sure Daddy was gone, and debated on whether or not to dial.

One quick phone call, I decided, and then I would take the phone downstairs to Daddy myself.

Just like he'd said he would, Travis clicked in from the other line. I was in my closet, with my back up against my shoe rack and my neck cradling the phone. "Hello?"

"Hi," I said, my voice strained from whispering.

"Who's this?" he asked. "Cassidy?"

"Yeah," I said in a whisper.

"You caught a cold?"

"No," I said.

"Your voice sounds funny. You okay?"

"It's probably this phone. A cordless."

"Oh. All right. Cool. So what's up?"

I settled into a more comfortable position. "Nothing."

"Where's Rik and G.?"

"They've gone home."

"I thought you guys were staying the night at Rik's? That's what Darwin said."

"Long story." I sighed.

"Oh."

"Yeah . . ."

"All right, so you never answered me," he said. "Skittles, Snickers, or Starburst?"

"Well," I said, "I don't really like chocolate, so—"

I was cut off by a dialing on the line, and then Daddy's voice. "Hello? Cassidy? Who's there?"

Travis said, "Hello? Cassidy?"

This was too incredibly awful. By now my heart was getting so used to racing that it could've tried out for the Olympics.

"Cassidy?" Daddy said. "Who are you talking to?"

I took a deep breath. "Daddy, I'll be off in a second."

"Even if you weren't on punishment, it's too late for you to be on the phone," he said. "Who's on the line?"

I couldn't believe this was happening! *"Daddy . . ."* I pleaded.

"Who's on the line?" Daddy shouted.

Travis hung up.

Great. Now Travis would think I was whack. I swore that

I would never leave the house again. Ever.

"Cassidy," Daddy said as the dial tone kicked in. "I want to see you downstairs in two seconds. Make that one." *Click.*

I hung up the phone. As I was coming out of the closet, I could hear Daddy downstairs warming up on his saxophone. A few uninspired notes morphed into a slow blues song. Definitely not a good sign.

"The important thing right now," Daddy said as I walked into the living room, "is that you understand how hard this is for me."

"Daddy, I—"

"Lying to me, calling boys late at night, and who knows what else?"

I swallowed.

"Maybe an all girls school is the best thing for you after all." He sighed.

"Daddy, no! Daddy, please, no. I swear. I won't—"

"A change of environment might be a good thing. We'll try it for a year, see how you—"

"I'll just run away," I interjected.

He looked at me. "*What did you say?*"

I stomped my foot. "I said I'll run away!" The tears wanted to flow, but I would not let them. And I did not bite down on my tongue, either. This was business. "Daddy, my worst enemy is going to Clara Ellis, and the only two friends I have are going to King. Do you want me to be miserable?"

"You're too young to even know what misery is. All you're going to do is focus on academics. No boys. No—"

"You want me to be a nerd! All the other girls my age talk to boys. I'm the only one who never knows what to say when a boy talks to me."

"There will be a time for all that, but not yet."

"Daddy, I'm almost thirteen," I said. "I'm *supposed* to be around boys."

"You're not thirteen *yet*," he said. "We have another month before we have to deal with that."

I started scraping the nail polish off my nails. For the first time, being twelve felt babyish.

"I'm sorry, pumpkin. But one day you'll thank me. It's the best school in the state. You'll be glad. You'll meet girls with goals."

"*Lane Benson* is going to that school, Daddy. And she wears a bikini, in front of boys!"

He cleared his throat. "Well, I don't know her. I'm not her father. But at least your cousin Tosha will be there. Maybe the two of you can—"

I screamed, "You can't do this to me, Daddy! You *cannot*. After everything we've been through? After I agreed to come live with you?"

"Six years from now," he said as he pulled his saxophone back to his mouth, "when you're going off to Spelman or some other fine university, you'll be glad you went to a college prep school."

I stormed out of the living room and was all the way up in my bedroom before I realized that Daddy was playing the white and gold saxophone out of Harmony's window. The one he'd been admiring for weeks. The one that I'd prayed for him to have.

Normally this would've made me happy, but right now I didn't think Daddy deserved such a nice thing. In fact, I was sorry I'd ever moved in with him. Who cared about Tosha? Who cared about college? Who cared about *anything* anymore?

August 27

Dear Mom,

I'm ready for you to come home. I don't like living with Daddy anymore, and I don't care if you get upset. He's making me go to Clara Ellis Academy, and it's ruining my life. I'm sick and tired of pretending like I'm so brave. I'm not. The truth is that I'm sad about the divorce. I wish that everything could just go back to the way it used to be. Even if it means you guys arguing all the time again, at least you'd be here.

The truth is that Rikki and I haven't gotten along so well this summer. Nothing is good anymore. Nothing! Maybe you won't even see me when you get back. Maybe I'll just run away.

Sixteen

It was the Saturday before Labor Day, the last weekend before school started, and Rikki was still on punishment. Aunt Honey agreed to let Golden and me stay the night, but only because we told her that we wanted to get up extra early and go to Sunday school. Daddy was taking me and Golden to the Labor Day weekend fireworks, and would drop us off at Rikki's afterward.

We both rode downtown in the backseat. Golden reached into the back pocket of her jean shorts and handed me an envelope. It was blue, and I immediately recognized all the stamps.

I held it close and smelled. "Mmm . . ."

"Isn't it cool?" Golden asked. "It reminds me of rain."

I sniffed again. "In a way it does," I said, and handed it back to her. "That's nice."

"I told Isabella about you," Golden said as she put the envelope back in her pocket. "She says she's got a friend that you can write to if you'd like."

"Really?"

"Yup. She just turned thirteen, our age."

"Okay, sure," I said. But I was still twelve, and I couldn't forget it.

Golden and I sat on a blanket, with Daddy in a folding chair behind us. The fireworks hadn't begun yet, and we were chatting away while Daddy read from one of his computer manuals. Things had really changed between Daddy and me since the pool party. He was more serious about being a better father than I'd ever imagined he was going to be. I was still sore at him, but deep down inside I also knew that it must be hard for him to have me stay so angry at him. That bothered me.

"Ray," we heard a female voice call. "Is that you?"

One look at her standing beside Daddy's chair, and instantly I knew who she was.

Tall. Model thin. Long, black spiral curls. Red lipstick. A cute little black dress. Who in their right mind wears high heels to see fireworks? Toni was absolutely disgusting.

Daddy chuckled, and I could tell that he was nervous.

"Well, well, well," he said. "Lookie here."

With her head titled to the side, the oogly woman grinned, and then she winked. She eyed me before she looked back at

Daddy. "And *this* must be your little girl. Cassidy, right?"

I snapped my eyes back to Daddy.

He scratched his eyebrow and laughed. Then he folded his hands across his chest and leaned back in his chair. "Yes, as a matter of fact. And, uh, also my neighbor's little girl, Golden."

"My," Toni said, batting her eyes. "They're adorable."

I folded *my* arms across *my* chest, too. "And who's this?" I asked.

Daddy twisted his neck and stretched until it made a popping sound. He started to say something, but a laugh came out instead.

Toni smiled a little too. "Protective, I see."

"Yeah," Daddy agreed. "That's my pumpkin."

Toni bent down and extended her hand for me to shake. A beautiful diamond bracelet was dangling from her wrist.

"Well," she said to me as if I was a four-year-old, "I'm Toni. And I'm a friend of your father's."

I let my hand go limp as she shook it, and I could tell by the expression on her face that she noticed.

Golden extended her hand next. "And I'm Golden. The neighbor's kid."

The way Golden rolled her eyes at me, I knew she didn't like Toni either.

Toni stood up again. "You ladies enjoy the show, okay?"

Daddy spoke on our behalf. "They will. Right, girls?"

Neither of us said a word.

Toni looked at Daddy. "They must be shy?"

He did that stupid chuckle that was starting to get on my nerves. "Uh, not really," he said.

"Oh." Toni sounded dry. Then she put her hand on her hip and tried to sound all energized again, all playful and friendly. "Well then, maybe they're just sizing me up? Is that what it is, girls? Maybe you'd like to see my resume, huh?"

I looked her up and down, and I could sense Golden doing the same.

Toni burst out laughing. "Ray, this is hilarious," she said. "They're too grown up for me."

Daddy did one of his dorky chuckles again.

"Well then." Toni winked. "Not to worry, girls. I just wanted to say hello. Good to see you, Ray," she added.

"Same here," Daddy replied.

"'Bye," I broke in.

I felt a little guilty about calling Ms. Carol's niece a chickenhead without really knowing her, but now, in a way, I was glad that Daddy *hadn't* mentioned her to me. I guess if he ever does mention a new lady friend, that'll mean that things are pretty serious. Thank goodness they're not, now that I've met Toni. Eeewwww.

"Ouch!" Golden yelped as Rikki finished French braiding her hair.

"Sorry," Rikki said. "Next time don't use any spritz before you come over."

Now Golden moaned as if she was disgusted. She continued

talking about the subject at hand. "My first stepdad was the worst. Well, they were both half-wits, but he used to smoke these awful cigars. Freddy's got asthma real bad, but he didn't care."

I grabbed a magazine and swung my legs over the arm of the La-Z-Boy.

Rikki held up a mirror so Golden could see how neat and pretty the braid going down her back was.

Golden stretched and craned her neck to see the reflection and smiled. "Cool," she said.

Rikki went over to the washing machine and reached behind it. When she came back, she put the box in the middle of the floor, and we gathered around and folded our legs.

"So," Rikki said. "What'd you bring?"

Golden reached over and grabbed her backpack off the couch. From it she pulled out a fancy gold box. Very carefully, she worked the red velvet bow off. And then she sat the box on the floor.

I read the script across the top. "Godiva," it said.

"Chocolate heaven in a box," Golden said. "But my mother says it's *full* of sinful calories."

"Good. Then it's definitely contraband," Rikki said.

Golden ran her fingers along the letters, her pink fingernail polish now old and chipped. "Guh-die-vuh," she pronounced the name.

Rikki laughed a little. "Looks more like 'go diva' to me."

Golden giggled too. "Hey, we could call it that," she said.

Rikki nudged me, "What do you think, Cass?"

I couldn't believe it. Rikki had finally used my nickname.

I nodded. "Right," I said. "I like that."

"Diva," Golden said. "It's kinda like saying you're cool, huh?"

"And that you're not gonna let anyone push you around," I said.

"Divas never do," Rikki said.

"And it's saying we're clever."

"And we've got style."

"And we're not nerdy."

"And the boys like us."

"The cute ones."

"The ones who are going places."

"Right."

"Right."

"Right."

We all laughed.

I thought for a second. "But that doesn't mean we're stuck-up, does it?"

Golden took a piece of candy out of the box. "Nope."

Rikki added, "Mary says there's a fine line between thinking highly of yourself and thinking you're all that."

"We must never cross that line," I said.

"Never."

"Never."

We all clinked pieces of chocolate together in the air.

I noticed Golden's hands again and said, "I could do your nails if you want."

Golden looked down at her nails, and I could tell that she hadn't realized how ragged they looked.

"Yes, please," Rikki said to Golden. "Let her."

"Okay."

The candy was so smooth, and the caramel in the middle was impossibly creamy. I couldn't *believe* how delicious it was. It was so good that I hummed as I chewed.

Tap. Tap.

Rikki groaned, got up, and ran over to the window. After Mary had pushed it open, she threw her sandals in first so as not to get mud on the table, and Rikki held her hands to help her in. The late night air came in with her, and Rikki hurried to close and re-lock the window. Soon it would be autumn.

Mary was smiling. "*¡Hola*, ladies!"

"*¡Hola!*" we replied.

"Whatever," Rikki snapped. "What took you so long?"

Mary took a deep breath as she went into the laundry room to change.

Rikki gave Golden a look as she joined us back in the circle. She whispered, "Watch when she comes back out—she's gonna try to act all romantic." Rikki called out to Mary, "This ain't *The Young and the Restless*, you know. You ain't Drucilla."

When Mary came back, now in her flowered pajamas and looking like she'd been in the basement the entire evening, she stood in front of our special box and let out a long sigh.

"Cassidy," Mary said with a soft smile, "I heard the news. Look at it this way, at least you're gonna get to write poems every day at school."

Golden and Rikki were looking at me sympathetically. We'd been avoiding the subject of school all evening.

Mary continued, "You should be happy that you're getting to go to one of the finest schools in the state. You'll get to study some of the finest poets that ever lived. Langston Hughes. Rita Dove. Walt Whitman. Jessica Care Moore. Emily Dickinson . . ."

"Good," I said. "Hopefully I'll have plenty of homework to keep me busy, since I'll probably never have fun again."

"Have you talked to Travis?" Mary wanted to know.

"No," I said. "I've had *nothing* all week. Today is my first day out of the house."

Mary fluttered her eyes and shook her head, "You'll see Travis again. Trust me, kiddo. When people care about each other, they find a way to stay in touch. You'll see."

Was that a tear in Mary's eye? I couldn't tell for sure.

"Yeah, Cass," Golden said. "Even friends."

"That's right," Rikki agreed. "Going to different schools will *never* keep us apart."

And still, Mary looked sad. Not caring what Rikki had to say or how she felt, I went ahead and said what I'd been wanting to say for a very long time. "Mary, you're my favorite poet."

Mary just laughed a little. "Yeah, well." She shook her

head. "That's real sweet of you to say, Cassidy. You're gonna do great at Clara Ellis."

I watched Mary as she meticulously wiped off her lip gloss with a Kleenex. And then, with a fat pink brush, she slowly wrapped her hair around her head. She tied it up with a silk scarf, looking so mellow and relaxed. Where in the *world* had she and Archie gone? What had they done?

Mary laughed. "Why are you guys looking at me like that?"

Rikki's nostrils were flared. "What happened tonight?" she demanded.

"Archie," Mary told us, "is such a gentleman."

Rikki gasped and acted like she was suffocating. "I'm gonna choke if you don't stop with the soap opera!"

Mary ignored her and said, "Listen to what I'm getting ready to tell you, okay, ladies?"

"We've been *listening*," Rikki interjected, "all the while since you got here. You ain't said nothing yet."

As usual Mary was not at all affected by Rikki's attitude. "Young ladies," she said, "have to be prepared. You never know. Just be ready, okay?"

With that, Mary dropped something inside the contraband box that landed with a soft thud. Rikki, Golden, and I peered over. Together we stared down into the land of smuggled goods, and then back at one another.

Both of my friends' eyes confirmed just what I was feeling. Complete and unimaginable shock. It was the kind of amazement that grabs you around the throat and makes it hard to swallow, makes you even forget how to do so, or even that you should.

Mary said, "Nobody ever did this for me, okay?"

In gym class Mrs. Watson had given us all pamphlets on sex and made us watch long movies about protection, but this was real life, not some woman in a polyester suit using big boring words. Touching one of those things would be a sin in itself. They were the ultimate contraband.

Surely Uncle Lance, who was upstairs sleeping, would awaken and beckon us to his throne a few miles down the road. We would kneel at the pulpit and repent for having thought of, looked at, and most definitely *touched* such a thing.

I sat motionless, ready to hear the sounds of Uncle Lance stirring upstairs. *Please don't let him wake*, I prayed.

Rikki said, "Times are different now. Hardly no one waits until marriage anymore."

Mary smiled. "It's okay to wait," she assured us. "Just, if you're ever ready, and you're *sure* you're ready, be *ready*, you know what I mean? Maybe you'll be someone who will wait until you get married. Good for you if you do."

Mary's words always had a way of making me feel better.

Then she ruined it. She started going on and on about diseases and getting pregnant, and all kinds of gross things. I just wanted her to stop, to shut up. I could not *believe* what she was saying. I was hoping, praying, that what Mary was talking about was not why she had snuck out tonight.

And whatever happened to Paul Bunyan?

"It's exactly what Daddy always preaches about." Mary sat down on the couch and clasped her hands together. "Our bodies are our temples, and we have to treat them with love and respect."

She continued, "*But*, when you truly care about someone, and when you're ready, it is the most exquisite thing imaginable. It's lovelier than the most colorful rainbow. More beautiful than a song by Alicia Keys."

Rikki reached in and held up one of the forbidden items like it was nothing but a piece of gum and then tossed it back in the box. She asked, "How are we supposed to know what to do with it?" She looked so comfortable touching it, like she'd seen one before, like she'd even *touched* one before for that matter. But we both had virgin eyes, and she knew it. All three of us did.

After Golden picked one up, I reached in too. But I dropped mine right back in. Immediately I tried to erase the memory of the way it felt. An airless balloon, suffocating in plastic. It landed on top of another, and they seemed to multiply. I counted. Mary had given us three.

"You just very *discreetly* give it to him." Mary's mouth rested into a calm pout as she thought for a moment, then she continued speaking in that motherly voice. "You don't say or do anything else. Just hand it to him. If he puts it on, you know he loves you. If he looks at you like he's mad, then get up and *get out*. Scream if you have to."

Mary leaned back and wrapped her arm across her stomach and around her waist, her hand holding onto her hip. She started tapping her fingers at her side and her usually dreamy eyes grew intense.

"Maybe it'll be years from now, maybe it won't, but whenever it happens, you are *never*," Mary instructed us, "to do the grown up without one. Comprende?"

"Sí." All three of us nodded.

From the smile on Rikki's face, I think even she would have agreed that having two friends is better than one. That night, the three of us promised to be together forever, no matter what. No crossing of hearts. No linking of pinky fingers. A promise has always been enough, and I know it always will be. Rikki, Golden, and me. The way things work even better.

September 12

Dear Mom,

Clara Ellis Academy for Girls. Wow! I can't believe it, but it's my new school.

My Intro to Poetry teacher is a young woman with short hair and a lovely laugh. Her name is Mrs. Rode, and she reminds me of the late Princess Diana of Wales and even speaks with an accent. On our first day she wrote on the chalkboard, "It takes a village to raise a child," and told us that this is an ancient African proverb, which made me think of you. In our notebooks, we were to write what we thought about that saying.

I wrote that it takes more than just a mom and a dad to help their kid through the tough times, and that maybe Forrest Hills is like a village, with plenty of help all around. Sometimes there is an uncle or an aunt, when a mom or dad can't be around. There are cousins, too, and friends, old and new.

The truth is that I miss you a whole lot, Mom, but it's okay that you're in Africa. I'll be right here waiting for you when you come home. I promise.

acknowledgments

To God be the glory. Thanks also to Leann Heywood, Mel Berger, Ali Douglass, Sasha Illingworth, Kathryn Silsand, Lisa Moraleda, Rockelle Henderson, Gilda Squire, and all of the wonderful experts at HarperCollins.

A newspaper article once misquoted my mother regarding what I'd asked for while shopping as a child. "It was always a book, never a Barbie," was how she was quoted. What my mother actually said was, "If it *wasn't* a book, it was a Barbie." I have such fond memories of what my friends called "BarbieLand" in my parents' basement. I still remember when my friends and I threw a big welcome-to-the-neighborhood Barbie party around the Barbie Swimming Pool, the Christmas when I received "The Heart Family," and even the plot where Ken saved Skipper from drowning. Mom and Dad, I know you could have done a lot of other things with what you spent on Barbies, but that's where a lot of my love for storytelling began. So thank you.

Here's to growing up in Toledo, the sorely missed Jacobson's and being on "J. Board," and Thackeray's Books. Here's to Dudley's, Southwyck Mall, Sleepy Hollow Park—better known as "The Pond"—the "Mini-Mac" on Dorr Street, and the Strawberry and the Old West End festivals. Here's to McTigue Junior High—and my "bestest friends" in the whole wide world back then. And here's especially to my three cousins who made growing-up adventures so fun. Nikeeta Ziegler, Joy Harrison, and Robyn Harrison—"Keeta-Bea," "Weez," and "Roddy."

My love and appreciation for their enduring support and/or encouragement: my sister Ginger, my family (far too many to name in the allotted space!), SUA, Marci Cannon, Rose Cannon, Rhonda B. Sewell (and *The Toledo Blade*), Chris Champion, Nkenge Abi, Stephanie Koehler, Melissa Timko, and Kelli Martin.

Finally, hello to my Leverette Junior High family in Toledo. Kids, *this one* you can read! Maybe Ms. Hawley will even give you a few extra credit points if you do!!